"Why didn't we meet when you were helping Dad?"

"I worked with him during the day," Lexie replied.

"While I worked the ranch and only came at night."

She smiled, remembering her favorite patient. "He talked about you a lot while we played chess, his favorite game, and he always beat me."

"He always beat me, too. Until near the end. But even then, he still wanted to play." Clint's voice was thick. "He was a great dad."

"And you were a great son."

He blinked, swiped his napkin across his eyes. "Let's go put that therapy equipment to good use. I want out of this chair. Especially if I'm supposed to walk my mom down the aisle anytime soon."

"Challenge accepted." Lexie stood and stuck Clint's plate in the dishwasher.

Had they just bonded? Not good. Not good at all.

She had to get this under control if she was going to be spending all day, every day with Clint. No bonding, no getting personally involved with and definitely no falling for the banged-up cowboy.

Shannon Taylor Vannatter is a stay-at-home mom, pastor's wife and award-winning author. She lives in a rural central Arkansas community with a population of around one hundred, if you count a few cows. Contact her at shannonvannatter.com.

Books by Shannon Taylor Vannatter

Love Inspired

Hill Country Cowboys

Hill Country Redemption
The Cowboy's Missing Memory

Texas Cowboys

Reuniting with the Cowboy
Winning Over the Cowboy
A Texas Holiday Reunion
Counting on the Cowboy

Love Inspired Heartsong Presents

Rodeo Ashes
Rodeo Regrets
Rodeo Queen
Rodeo Song
Rodeo Family
Rodeo Reunion

Visit the Author Profile page at Harlequin.com.

The Cowboy's Missing Memory

Shannon Taylor Vannatter

Recycling programs for this product may not exist in your area.

ISBN-13: 978-1-335-48827-5

The Cowboy's Missing Memory

This edition published by arrangement with Harlequin Books S.A.

For questions and comments about the quality of this book, please contact us at CustomerService@Harlequin.com.

Love Inspired
22 Adelaide St. West, 40th Floor
Toronto, Ontario M5H 4E3, Canada
www.Harlequin.com

Printed in U.S.A.

These things I have spoken unto you,
that in me ye might have peace. In the world
ye shall have tribulation: but be of good cheer;
I have overcome the world.

—*John* 16:33

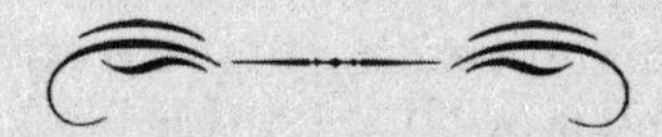

To our family and church family. I don't know what we'd have done without y'all this past year.

Acknowledgments

I'm thankful to my second cousin, Regan Payne, for introducing me to the field of occupational therapy and breathing life into my heroine and story line for this book.

Chapter One

On her way out, Lexie Parker glanced toward the ER.

Audrey Rawlins paced the waiting room.

Stopping Lexie in her tracks. A knot developed in her stomach and sank. Gathering her courage, she sat the good-bye plant from her coworkers on a bench, pushed the red button to open the door and hurried to the woman she'd let down two and a half years ago.

"Audrey?"

"Oh, Lexie." Audrey hugged her, sobs deep, shaken to her core.

"What's happened?"

"It's my son, Clint," the other woman squeaked out. "Bull wreck."

Still riding bulls? After what happened to his dad? How could he be so selfish to put his mom through this?

"Here. Sit down." Lexie eased Audrey back to a chair. "I'll go see what I can find out."

"Oh, would you?" Audrey sank down in the seat, pulling her coat tighter around her shoulders.

"Of course." She gave the distraught woman's hands a squeeze. "I'll be right back." With leaden legs, she hurried to the nurses' window. "Clint Rawlins is a friend." Though she'd never actually met him. "Could you let me back?"

The nurse nodded and the automatic door crept open. As soon as the opening was wide enough to slip past, Lexie darted through. And almost took out Mandy Hopkins.

"Girl, where's the fire? I thought you were out of here. It's midnight on Saturday. Go have some fun."

At midnight, Lexie's idea of fun was her warm bed. "The bull wreck patient, Clint Rawlins—do you know anything about his condition?"

"You know him?"

"I know his mom." And his dad had been her favorite patient. "She's currently beside herself."

"Let me see what I can find out."

"Thanks. I'll be with her in the waiting room." Lexie retraced her steps, pushed the red button to open the door and waited until it was fully open this time.

Audrey rushed her. "Is he okay?"

"We should know something soon. I sent one of my nurse friends to get details."

"The last time I was here was with his father." She shuddered.

"I know." Lexie clasped the woman's shoulder and uttered a silent prayer, *Please, God, let Clint be okay. History can't repeat itself.*

"I thought he quit after his dad got sick. But he's so stubborn. Like father, like son." Audrey mopped her face, a stoic strength settling the lines in her face.

The ER door opened and Mandy popped out. "He's stable. And awake for the moment. He has a severe concussion, but there's no brain swelling and no bleeds, so that's good. Dr. Arnett ordered more tests, but y'all can come back and see him for a few minutes if you'd like."

"Oh, thank you, Jesus." Audrey hugged Lexie.

Relief whooshed through her, leaving her weak and sagging as she managed to land uncoordinated pats on Audrey's back. Her son was alive.

"Are you coming?" Clint's mom stood. "I always wanted the two of you to meet."

"I doubt he feels much like making new acquaintances right now." But Audrey shouldn't face this alone. "You go on, I'll be there in a minute." Lexie snagged Mandy's wrist as another nurse escorted Clint's mom to his room. "Any brain damage?" Her question came out hesitant, as she feared the answer.

"The preliminary tests show frontal lobe damage. He'll probably need rehab. It's a shame this was your last day."

"Any other injuries? Broken bones?"

"The only part of him the bull stepped on was his head."

Her knees almost buckled; nausea threatened.

"Whoa." Mandy grabbed her hands and pulled her toward a waiting room chair. "Who is this guy to you?"

"No one. I mean—I never met him. But his dad was my patient. The first one I—"

"You lost." Mandy patted her back. "I think you missed the day when your instructor went over keeping a professional distance. But your compassion is what makes you a great occupational therapist."

Yes, she'd gotten too close to him, and to Audrey. She ducked her head. "Levi had a degenerative brain disease from too many bulls stepping on his head. I helped him learn to feed himself and walk again, but within six months, he was gone." Her mouth went dry. She just didn't want to see Audrey relive it all again. She'd been through enough already.

"Mr. Rawlins was wearing a helmet. If he hadn't been, he wouldn't be here. But the helmet cracked. We'll know more once all the tests are done."

"You'll keep me posted?"

"Of course." Mandy motioned the nurse on duty to open the door for her.

Lexie took several deep breaths, straightened her spine,

eyed her plant. So much packing to do. But even with her impending move, Audrey needed her.

Frontal lobe injury could mean a whole host of things. Impaired speech, trouble with fine motor skills, balance, memory, mood swings, personality changes—the list went on. Who would Clint be when he woke up?

She scooped up her plant, set it in the nurses' window. "Can you watch this for me and let me back again?"

"Sure." The duty nurse let her through and she quickly found Audrey camped by her son's bed in a curtained cubicle.

Clint was still unconscious, his face slack and relaxed. Unmarred, handsome, amazingly unscathed. How did a person even survive a bull stepping on their head? She scanned the monitors as they beeped and pulsed. Good readings. No intubation. All positive signs.

"The nurse said he was awake, but he was out again by the time I got here," Audrey whispered. "When do you think he'll wake up again?"

"It could be any time."

"Aren't they supposed to keep you awake when there's a concussion?"

"That's if you leave the hospital. He's in good hands here." Lexie stood. "I should go. Some stranger isn't the first thing he should see when he wakes. I can meet him once he's feeling better."

"I saw your mom at church and she told me this is your last week here. It's a shame you're not in the rehabilitation center anymore." Audrey turned sad eyes on her. "The doctor said he'll probably have to spend some time there."

"The new therapist is really good. You'll like him." She'd keep tabs on Clint's recovery, even though she wouldn't be his OT.

"It won't be the same, though." Audrey sighed, then

stood to give her a hug. "So you're moving back to Medina? With your parents?"

"Until I can find a place of my own." With a much-needed, month-long sabbatical before she'd go to work at the rehab center close to her hometown. No more apartment in San Antonio. With the savings she'd put aside, and the dent she'd put in her student loans, she'd be able to afford her own rental house.

"At least we'll be neighbors."

"I'm looking forward to seeing you outside of this place." Lexie checked Clint's monitors for the umpteenth time, then studied his features. The man's sun-bronzed complexion showed through his pallor, and his strong jaw bristled with dark stubble.

His eyes popped open. She froze. Vivid green eyes, so like his dad's, latched on to her.

"Oh, son, you're awake." Mom leaped from her chair and rushed to his side.

"Where am I?" He frowned, squinted, trying to push the haze in his brain aside.

"You're in the hospital." A slight quiver in the nurse's voice. Familiar. Standard burgundy scrubs. Dark hair and eyes. Pretty. Where had he seen her?

"What happened?" His words slurred. And his head hurt. Really badly.

"A bull, that's what." Mom perched on the side of his bed.

"Oh, yeah." Clint closed his eyes. He was so busted. "I didn't want you to know. Didn't want you to worry."

"It's a little late for that." The worry in her eyes tugged at him.

"I'm sorry, Mom. There's no excuse for letting you find out this way. But this was my last ride. I made the buzzer, just failed on my dismount. I should have made enough tonight to save the ranch."

"The ranch is fine." Mom frowned. "You promised me you'd quit."

"I meant to. But I couldn't let you lose the ranch. Not after Dad worked so hard to build it. We couldn't lose his legacy six months after losing him."

Mom let out a little gasp.

"Sometimes things are a little fuzzy at first." The nurse gave Mom's shoulder a soothing pat and scrutinized him. "Do you know what day it is, Mr. Rawlins?"

"Of course." But he couldn't come up with it. "Well, maybe not exactly. But it's toward the end of February. The last night of the San Antonio Stock Show and Rodeo."

"That's right. But what year?"

"It wasn't that hard a knock." He closed his eyes, rattled off the year.

Mom clamped her hand over her mouth.

"What?"

"We should let him rest and I'll consult with his doctor. Let him know he's awake." The nurse motioned Mom toward the door and turned away. "Your mom will be back later."

And it hit him where he'd seen her. Dad's funeral.

Mom turned and clasped his hand. "They'll probably run me out of here soon anyway." Her tone came out an octave too high. "I wasn't supposed to stay long."

He focused on her hand. Her wedding rings were gone. A solitary diamond ring in their place. "What's this? Where are Dad's rings?"

Mom had that deer-caught-in-the-headlights look as she pulled her hand away.

Why was she acting so weird? Something was very wrong here.

Chapter Two

Clint was stuck two years in the past. Lexie bit her lip. She'd heard of cases like this. Had actually done OT work with patients suffering from memory lapses. And the doctor always said it was best to ease into catching the patient up to speed.

"My wedding rings are at the jeweler getting cleaned," Audrey covered, as if the engagement ring gracing her finger wasn't there.

"Your doctor needs to know you're awake." Lexie tugged Audrey away from his bedside. "Come on," she said, scurrying his mom out the door.

"What's going on? He got the year wrong." Audrey's voice quivered. "By two years. And he thinks Levi died six months ago instead of two and a half years."

"Sometimes, with head injuries, a patient can experience a time lapse. I need you to go to the waiting room and I'll find his doctor."

"It's temporary?" Audrey frowned.

"Most of the time," Lexie answered, pushing the red button that opened the door to the waiting room. As Audrey stepped through, Lexie noticed a frantic man hurrying toward them.

"Oh, Ted, I'm so glad you're here." Audrey rushed into his arms.

Ah, the fiancé attached to the ring. Lexie felt better about leaving Audrey in his hands. The door closed and she caught up with Mandy.

"Hey, can you tell Dr. Arnett that Clint Rawlins is awake? He seems to be having some memory issues, though. I'd like to fill him in on the conversation he just had with his mom."

"Sure." Mandy dashed away.

Lexie leaned against the wall, hugging herself.

"Lexie." Dr. Arnett's shoes squeaked across the polished floor. "Come to the consultation room and tell me what's going on."

She followed, doing her best to keep up with the busy doctor's sprint. He ushered her inside, then shut the door. The room with soft aqua walls, healthy plants and calming artwork was designed to soothe nerves. But it wasn't working for Lexie.

"You know Mr. Rawlins?"

She quickly caught him up on how she knew of him and went on to explain about Clint's confusion.

"Now that you brought me up to speed, I remember having his father as a patient. Hmm..." Dr. Arnett scanned the file he held. "With the head injury he sustained, it's quite common for memory issues to occur." He closed the file. "Any significant happenings in the last two years of his life?"

"His mom is supposed to get married in a few months." She'd gotten the invitation, sent her RSVP and marked her calendar. "And his sister was visibly pregnant at his dad's funeral, so I assume he's an uncle again. I think she already had a son."

"I see." The doctor stood. "Thanks for the heads-up.

Since you'll know what he has right and wrong to a certain degree, why don't you come along for my chat with him?"

"Of course."

With leaden legs, she stood, as well, then followed the doctor to Clint's room.

"I heard you were awake." Dr. Arnett checked the monitors and computer by Clint's bed. "I'm Stan Arnett, head neurologist."

"When can I get out of here, doc?"

"Not so fast, young man. You don't get your head stepped on by a bull and live to tell about it very often."

"Wow, that's what happened? I don't remember."

"I imagine not. Tell me what you do remember. About your life for the last few years."

"My dad was sick for a year and a half. I spent most of that time helping my mom care for him. He died six months ago." Clint closed his eyes, as if the loss was really that fresh.

"What about since your dad's passing?" Dr. Arnett typed something into the computer.

"I found out my mom's ranch was in financial trouble, so I competed in the San Antonio Stock Show and Rodeo event to raise the money to catch up on the loan payments. Bull riding caused my dad's illness and I didn't want my mom to worry, so I didn't tell her what I was up to." His guilty gaze sank to the floor. "But tonight was my last ride. I made it eight seconds and my earnings will put the ranch back in the black."

"So you remember the ride?" Dr. Arnett asked.

Clint nodded. "But not the dismount."

A bad sign. But since he'd lost consciousness, not unexpected.

"And what date is it?"

Clint frowned in concentration, then came up with February 23. A few days short and still two years behind on the year.

"And how old are you?" the doctor probed.

"Twenty-six."

But Lexie was pretty sure he was twenty-eight.

"All right." Dr. Arnett checked the computer, then stepped away from the bed. "You get some rest."

"Can the nurse stay?" Clint focused on Lexie. "I've seen you before and it's driving me up the wall trying to place you."

"This is Lexie Parker, our former cccupational therapist. And we're all wishing it wasn't former. You're stable, so you don't need a nurse. We'll be moving you into a regular room soon." The doctor hurried for the door. "It's late and you need rest."

"But wait." He reached toward her. "I know you, Lexie. You were at my dad's funeral."

"Yes, that's right." Of all the things to remember with his muddled brain…

"You were his therapist. Mom bragged on you. Said Dad's last days wouldn't have been as functional without you. That he wouldn't have been able to spend them at home if not for you. I've always wanted to thank you."

"I'm glad I could help him." Her vision clouded. "Don't tell my other patients, but Levi was my favorite." She gave him a finger wave and exited. Glad she was behind the doctor, she blinked the moisture away and focused.

"We'll go back to the consultation room. I just texted a nurse to get his mom so she can join us." Dr. Arnett ushered her in front of him as they retraced their steps, then closed the door behind them.

"How long until he regains his memory?" Lexie settled in one of several chairs lining the room.

"Each case is unique, but most of the time, within a few weeks."

"Could his memory loss be permanent?"

"It could happen, but it's rare." A knock sounded on the door. "Come in."

A nurse opened the door, and a nervous-looking Audrey and Ted stepped inside, along with a very pretty blonde woman probably close to Lexie's age. Clint's girlfriend, perhaps?

"Please, have a seat." He opened Clint's file. "I'm Dr. Arnett, head of neurology. I'm familiar with the Rawlins family since Levi was my patient."

"Then you remember Audrey, Clint's mom." Ted kept his arm around her shoulders. "And her daughter, Carly. I'm Audrey's fiancé."

Oh, yes. Lexie remembered Carly from the funeral. She'd been pregnant. And brunette.

"I asked Lexie along for my consultation, since she's familiar with your family, as well."

"Lexie was Levi's occupational therapist. A true blessing." Audrey's smile quivered.

"I saw you at Dad's funeral, but I'm so glad to finally meet you." Carly shook Lexie's hand.

"You, too."

"What exactly are we dealing with here, Doc?" Ted's grimace revealed his worry.

"Clint has lost the last two years. He believes he's twenty-six and his father died six months ago."

"Why two years, I wonder?" Audrey asked.

"The mind is a tricky thing. But looking into his medical history, I found he woke up after a bull wreck in our emergency room almost exactly two years ago, with a concussion. It looks like his brain has taken him back to that time."

"A bull wreck? Two years ago?" Audrey shook her head. "That's impossible."

"Our records indicate it was a minor concussion and we kept him overnight for observation."

"How could I not know that?" She sank further into her seat. "I thought he quit bull riding after Levi's diagnosis."

"Actually—" Carly's eyes squeezed closed "—he competed in the rodeo at San Antonio two years ago. To save the ranch. He didn't tell me until he ended up here. In fact, I'm the one who drove him home from the ER the next morning. But he promised me he wouldn't do it again."

As family secrets spilled, Lexie felt more and more out of place.

"He won that money riding bulls?" Audrey shook her head. "He told me y'all cashed in the savings bonds Grandpa left."

"We did, but they weren't enough."

"I should have known." Audrey's eyes widened. "He had a concussion then and now a brain injury." She released a shuddering breath. "Please tell me he won't end up like Levi."

"We'll know more when we get more tests back. But Levi's illness isn't hereditary."

"But it was a result of bull riding." Carly blew out a big breath.

"Yes, but let's not get ahead of ourselves." Dr. Arnett used his best soothing tone. "Your father competed in the rodeo for much longer and had a lot more bull wrecks under his belt than your brother."

"Could Clint end up with other problems?" Carly asked.

"He might have some issues with balance, motor skills, hand-eye coordination. We'll know more once we get him on his feet in the morning."

"But this is all fixable?" Audrey hung on every word. "Right?"

"In all probability, the memory problems will clear up in a week or two, a few months at most. I will caution you, though. Injuries like this often cause changes in personality, most notably mood swings and temper tantrums. Sometimes even violent episodes. If we see anything like that, I'll have a neurophysiologist consult with him."

"What's that?" Audrey's gaze pinged from Dr. Arnett to Lexie.

"A specialist who assesses reasoning impairment." Lexie tried to give a layman's definition. "And helps the patient manage behaviors and learn coping methods."

"So what's our course of action?" Ted asked, in take-charge mode.

The more Lexie saw of him, the more she liked him.

"In my experience, patients recover more quickly if they're calm and relaxed. So I recommend that you help him recapture memories slowly. Start with gently explaining what year it is. Once that's sunk in for him, Audrey can explain her relationship with you. Let him chew on that a few days before you show up."

"You want us to lie to him?" Clint's mom scoffed.

"In the interest of helping him make a full, frustration-free recovery, yes. Just for a few days, a week at the most."

Lexie caught Audrey's gaze and gave her a reassuring smile. "If you dump everything on him at once, he might feel overwhelmed."

Audrey blew out a big sigh. "So Ted needs to stay clear?"

"Yes. Clint thinks his father has only been gone for six months. His mom having a fiancé would be very jarring for him."

"I'll do whatever's best for Clint." Ted's jaw set in a stubborn line. "But I can't just sit back and let Audrey deal with this alone."

"You need to steer clear of Clint, not his mom," Dr. Arnett said with a smile.

"What about the wedding in six weeks, do we need to postpone?"

"Oh, Ted. No." Audrey clutched his arm.

"It's okay. Right now, we need to do what's best for your boy."

Lexie's heart squeezed, thankful Audrey had found a second selfless man to love her.

"Don't do anything rash about the wedding," the doctor advised. "He could remember everything by this time next week."

"How long will he have to stay here?" Audrey asked.

"We're still waiting on a few test results, but he should be able to go home in a few days."

"But the wedding invitations have gone out. If he talks to anyone who knows, he'll find out," Ted reasoned.

Dr. Arnett cleared his throat. "You'll need to keep him secluded until he's up to speed on all the major changes he's forgotten."

"And you're certain this is the best course of action?" Audrey clasped shaky hands in her lap.

"Hopefully, by the end of the week, he'll remember everything on his own. Maybe a few weeks."

"All right, then, I'll disappear until I get the all clear," Ted agreed.

Carly stood, her flat stomach apparent in a slim-fitting dress, reminding Lexie of the difference since the last time she'd seen Clint's sister.

"There's one more thing. How many children do you have now, Carly?" Lexie asked.

"Oh, that's right. Two years ago, I was huge—Charlee wasn't born yet. And Cooper was five."

Audrey covered her face with both hands. "How do we tell him he has a niece who will be two in a month and a nephew who's seven instead of five like he remembers?"

Dr. Arnett tapped his chin with an index finger. "You and your brother are close?"

"Very." Carly shrugged. "I mean we give each other a hard time, but we're pretty tight. And he's very close to my son, Cooper, too."

"After you let him in on the time lapse, let him remember the pregnancy on his own and then explain. And don't bring your son to see him until he's had time for it all to sink in."

"But what if he gets his thoughts together enough to notice I'm no longer pregnant before we tell him about the past two years?"

"Just be gentle with him," Dr. Arnett assured her. "You'll know what to say when the time comes."

Audrey dabbed her nose with a fresh tissue. "What about therapy?"

"Once he's up to speed on the last two years, we can get him a room in our PT facilities or send a therapist to him. I think you'll like our occupational therapist."

"He'll never agree to stay here." Audrey shook her head. "He needs to be home."

"Order whatever equipment he needs." Ted patted Audrey's shoulder. "I'll pay for everything."

"That's very kind. But the cost could be exorbitant even with rental equipment," Dr. Arnett cautioned.

"I'm good for it. I didn't mention my last name, did I? Ted Townsend."

As in Townsend Gas & Oil. Yeah, he was definitely good for it, Lexie noted. And very generous.

"If you're certain that's what you want?"

"Anything for Audrey's boy." Ted turned to Lexie. "Since you know your stuff, can you oversee ordering the equipment he'll need?"

"That's too much to ask," Clint's mom interrupted. "Lexie is trying to get moved and she has a new job."

"Actually, my job doesn't start for a month and I'd like to help."

"All right, with Lexie's help, I'll get the equipment ordered." Dr. Arnett closed the file. "I'll also compile a list of therapists in the area to contact so you can set up a schedule to work with him daily."

"Actually, I'm hoping we have our therapist." Audrey grabbed Lexie's hand. "It's like God put this together for us. You between jobs and my son needing you."

Her heart turned over. "Let me think about it." An opportunity to help the Rawlins family. To guide Clint to a full recovery—the thing she couldn't do for his dad. Was this her second chance to make things right for this family?

"When should we break it to Clint about his lost years?" Carly asked.

"Tomorrow morning. We'll see how he takes the news, get all the test results, and go from there on when to release him." The doctor checked his watch.

Ted took the hint and stood. "We'll let you get back to your other patients."

As the family filed out, Lexie's heart hurt for them. Despite Dr. Arnett's assurances that Clint would probably fully recover, fear lingered in Audrey's eyes. Making Lexie want to do whatever she could to ease her worries.

It took all of Clint's concentration to take one step. Drenched in sweat, he managed one toddler-sized, wobbly step, with Willis, the orderly, supporting the bulk of his weight.

"Why won't my feet do what I tell them to?"

"Maybe because a bull—which you weren't supposed to be riding—stepped on your head." Carly harrumphed, dwarfed by her billboard-sized purse.

"It's good to see you too, sis."

"You're doing fine." The orderly settled him back in his chair and typed something into the computer.

"I have every right to be quite livid." Carly tapped her foot. "You almost got yourself killed last night."

"But he didn't." Mom shot his sister *the look*. "This is no time for anger. We need to count our blessings that Clint came out as unscathed as he did."

"Where's Joel? I need my brother-in-law to take my side."

Carly hesitated, drawing in a shaky breath. "He got deployed to Afghanistan."

"*Afghanistan?* When?"

"He'll be back in a month."

"That's a short little deployment. Oh, I get it. They're letting him come home for the baby's birth."

Mom and Carly looked at each other, then gave him an encouraging smile.

Something was up with them. "When do I get to start therapy? Where's Lexie?"

"Dr. Arnett didn't say." Mom shrugged. "And I imagine she's packing."

"Packing?"

"Yesterday was Lexie's last day here. She's got a new job at the rehab center in Bandera."

So once he got out of here, would she be his therapist? Why did it matter to him? Because she'd been so instrumental in Dad's treatment?

Carly turned his chair toward the door.

"Am I out of here?"

"Not quite. Dr. Arnett said we can take you outside for some fresh air," she answered.

"Sounds like just what the doctor ordered." Willis typed something else in the computer. "How about lunch outside?"

"Sure." But Clint longed to see what he'd written. Just how bad off was he?

Carly wheeled him out of his room, down the corridor to a set of double doors. It hurt his pride to have his big sister compensating for his inability to mobilize his wayward limbs.

But once they got outside, he could breathe better. Maybe even think better.

She parked him under a large live oak tree and Willis hooked a tray holding his lunch on his chair. The two women in his life settled on a bench facing him. Mom looked like she had when they'd had to tell him his dog died, when he was eight.

"What's going on?"

"Eat your lunch, sweetheart. We just have a few things to discuss."

"How bad off am I?" He homed in on Carly. She wouldn't sugarcoat it.

"All things considered, you're in pretty good shape. You'll need occupational therapy to help you regain your balance and fine motor skills. And…there are a few holes in your memory." She turned to their mom.

"What? I remember everything but my dismount." Didn't he? Something twisted in his stomach.

"Honey, it's not a big deal." Mom's tone was all soft, as if she were speaking to a child. "The doctor says it happens all the time with brain injuries. And your memory should come back just fine."

Except for one thing. That was how Dad's illness began. With memory loss.

He frowned. "Is there something I don't know?" His gaze fastened on his sister's midsection. She was supposed to be pregnant. Wasn't she? Had she had another miscarriage? Then the reason for her huge purse dawned on him. She'd been hiding behind it. "Oh, sis, did you lose the baby?"

She gasped. "No! I had her, a little girl—Charlee. She's fine."

"Oh, thank You, God." He closed his eyes. Think. Think. "So you had her while I was in the ER?"

"It seems you've lost a couple of years." Mom told him the date and year. Two years in the future.

"What?" His brain crashed.

"It's been two and a half years since Dad died." Carly knelt beside him, squeezing his hand.

"Two and a half years?" No…that was impossible. "It's only been six months."

Carly pulled a newspaper out of her purse and handed it to him.

He read the date. February 26. He'd been close. But the year took his breath away. His head hurt. Badly. How could he lose two years of his life? The newspaper slipped from his grip. The wind caught it, separated it and strewed sections across the lawn. Just like the scattered pieces of his mind.

"Clint. Sweetheart. Are you okay?" Mom's voice sounded far away.

"I'd like to go back to my room now."

Chapter Three

Church had been a blur, but Lexie had gone to the altar to pray for Clint and put him on the prayer list. As she navigated the hospital parking lot, the afternoon sun warmed things up a bit, but the air still had a bite to it.

She met patients hobbling around or in wheelchairs, family members tending to them, nurses and doctors obviously at the end of their shifts, yawning their way toward the parking garage. As she neared the building, a familiar form caught her eye—Carly sitting on a bench, staring at the water fountain.

"You okay?"

The young woman let out a harsh, derisive laugh. "I really couldn't tell you."

"Is Clint okay?" Lexie held her breath. *Please, Lord, how much can one family take?*

"He's resting. Mom's up in his room with him, and Ted's in the waiting room—pretending he doesn't exist. Clint's probably getting released tomorrow afternoon and we're supposed to meet in Dr. Arnett's office to go over his test results in a few minutes." Releasing a heavy sigh, Carly tucked her hair behind her ears. "I had to come out here to call and check on the kids since I couldn't get a good signal inside."

"I know this is hard."

"This morning, we told him he'd lost two years." Carly let out a weary sigh.

"How did he take it?"

"He's frustrated, upset. Imagine how you'd feel if you woke up missing two years." She dabbed her eyes with a mascara-smeared tissue. "I've never seen him like that. So lost, so confused. Just like the beginning of Dad's illness. When we didn't know what was going on yet."

"I know it must seem like history repeating itself, but there's no reason to think your brother has your dad's disease." Lexie tried to sound confident and reassuring. "It's not hereditary and your brother's rodeo career has lasted a much shorter time than your dad's. With therapy, he should make a complete recovery."

"Have you thought about taking the job? With my husband deployed, I'm pulling double duty with the kids, plus my job at the bank. I can't be there for Mom like I want to be." Carly stared into the fountain. "It would be such a huge relief to Mom to have someone she knows and trusts working with Clint."

The fountain's soothing spray created white noise and usually mesmerized the senses, eased worries. But today, it failed to calm Lexie's zinging nerves.

"I'm here because your mom wants me to see the results, so I'll know exactly what Clint will require."

"Oh, Lexie, thank you." Carly hugged her.

"I haven't agreed."

"I know. But you haven't said no, either."

And it would be hard for her to say no to Audrey. Why did Clint's sister have such faith in her?

"Our family's just been through so much," Carly confided, wringing her hands. "And we're all so worried Clint will end up like Dad. But you helped Dad."

"The two cases are completely different. And despite my help, your father—"

"Still died." Carly patted her hand. "That wasn't your fault. He was terminal and we all knew it. But you gave him his dignity back. Because of you, he spent his last months mobile and self-sufficient instead of depending on us for every little thing. That was priceless to him."

"Thank you." Lexie's throat clogged up. "That means a lot to me."

Carly sighed. "I know the new therapist is great. We met him last night and Dr. Arnett gave us a list of in-home therapists. But Mom and I would feel so much better with someone we know and trust focused solely on Clint full-time. I hate to pressure you, but I don't know if Mom will have any peace unless you're his therapist."

Even though Levi's disease had been terminal, since he'd been Lexie's patient, she'd taken his death personally. Especially since he'd been the first patient she lost. She almost felt she owed Audrey to work with Clint. To somehow make up for Levi's death.

What would she do for a month without work anyway? It wasn't like she had a personal life.

"Okay. I'm in."

"Really?" Carly hugged her. "Thank you! Mom will be so relieved."

The two women stood, walked arm in arm to the hospital and took an elevator up. They met up with Ted in the waiting room.

"Where's Mom?"

"In with Clint. Dr. Arnett just went to summon her for our meeting." Ted turned to Lexie. "Could I speak with you for a moment?"

"Of course." She followed him to a corner.

"I admire your field of work." He lowered his voice.

"Not to be nosy, but I imagine your degree probably racked up a sizable student loan."

She widened her eyes. What was he getting at? "I was able to get some scholarships, but the reason I stayed in San Antonio so long was to whittle down what I owe."

"I certainly don't mean to imply that you can be bought, Ms. Parker. But I'll do anything for Audrey, and I'm prepared to pay off your debt if you'll take on Clint as a patient."

Her heart warmed.

"I'll do anything for Audrey, as well. I've actually already told Carly I'll take the job. A normal salary will suffice and we can talk about it later."

"But there's no time like the present. I got some prices from other in-home therapists this morning, ran some numbers." He handed her a slip of paper. "Does this seem fair?"

She glanced down. Almost exactly what she owed, with a few dollars to spare. "That's way too much."

"I can assure you, it's the going rate for in-home OT care."

Well, in that case, this had to be a God thing. Affirmation that she'd made the right decision.

"Perhaps after you complete your work with Clint, you might want to switch to in-home care."

"No. It's never been about the money for me."

"Which is precisely why we want you." Ted smiled.

"Ah, Lexie." Dr. Arnett escorted Audrey into the waiting room. "Glad you're here. Now that we're all accounted for, let's gather in my office."

The family followed.

Though it was a sizable office, by the time they'd all filed in, it was almost standing room only.

Dr. Arnett pulled a file and put the X-rays on the lighted screen. "This is the frontal lobe, the part of Clint's brain that's affected," he said, indicating with his pointer. "It controls thought processes, decision-making, emotions. What was his reaction when you told him what year it is?"

"Disbelief." Carly swallowed hard. "Until I showed him a newspaper."

"And then he was eerily calm," Audrey said. "He just wanted to go back to his room."

"From the conversation I had with him this afternoon, Clint is frustrated." Dr. Arnett crossed his arms. "His father's death is very fresh for him. He feels like he wasn't there for y'all in the aftermath and he hasn't been around for your kids, Carly."

"But he has been."

"Yet he doesn't remember being there," the doctor reiterated. "Over the next week or so, I want you to show him pictures of everything that took place over the last two years. Especially of him with Audrey and with the kids. That will give him a bright spot and he'll realize that he was in fact there for everyone."

"In my experience," Lexie said, patting Audrey's arm, "most patients improve greatly just by getting to go home to familiar surroundings." Maybe everything would click into place for Clint and he'd only need her for his physical issues.

"And you're releasing him tomorrow?" The older woman gripped the seat of her chair, leaned forward, head down, as if steeling her strength. Or maybe even praying.

"It may be later in the day, but yes," Dr. Arnett confirmed. "He needs rest, people who love him and a good therapist. Once things sink in for him, bring the kids to see him. And then after he adjusts, you can break the engagement news, Audrey. But Ted, you need to give him plenty of time to get used to the idea of you before you become part of his picture."

"I'll do whatever's best for Clint," Ted agreed.

"For today, I think it might be best if y'all go home."

Dr. Arnett turned the light of the X-ray screen off. "Clint is on emotional overload. I prescribed a sedative and he'll sleep until morning. Besides, I doubt any of you have slept much since he was brought in here."

"I can't leave him here all alone," Audrey said, shaking her head.

Lexie stood. "I'll sit with him."

"Would you?" His mom sighed. "That would make us feel better."

"Of course. He's my patient."

Audrey clasped a hand to her heart. "You're taking the job."

"How could I say no to you?"

"Oh, thank you," Audrey breathed, her eyes tearing up. "An answered prayer."

"Since he's my patient, I need y'all to fill me in on everything you know about Clint's life that might be helpful to me. Do you know why he was riding bulls again?"

"I'm guessing to raise the money to buy a beefalo ranch in Fort Worth," Audrey volunteered.

Ted's gaze dropped to the floor. "And I'm guessing that even though he gave us his blessing, it was hard seeing his mama with somebody who wasn't his daddy. And that's why he was in such an all-fired hurry to move to Fort Worth."

"But he thinks the world of you, Ted," Audrey assured her fiancé.

"I know, but he still misses his daddy. Especially now. Maybe we rushed things. Maybe we should have given him more time to get used to us."

"I don't think he wanted to move to get away from y'all." Carly shifted in her seat. "He wanted to make his own way instead of hanging around and being y'all's third wheel. He wanted Ted to feel at home at the ranch 'cause he knew Mama would never leave it."

"This is good," Lexie said. "I apologize for being nosy, but if I'm to help Clint emotionally and physically, I need to understand the dynamics of his life. So there wasn't any upheaval except for his dad's death?"

"And me stealing his mama away."

"Here's what we're not gonna do." Lexie went into therapist mode. "We're not gonna play the blame game. Clint isn't a child. I doubt he'd want the rest of y'all putting your lives on hold on his behalf. Was he glad to see you happy again, Audrey?"

"Yes."

"And he approved of Ted?"

"That's right."

"Then we're going to work on his physical problems and mobility issues along with easing his emotional upheaval and helping him recover his memories. And no one's going to blame themselves. We're going to blame the bull. Okay?"

"Okay." All family members echoed their agreement.

"Once he's ready to know about Ted, let him remember how he felt about everything on his own," Lexie said, making eye contact with each family member. "Let him recover his reasons for wanting to move to Fort Worth. The main thing you need to do is be careful of swaying his feelings with how you think he feels."

Dr. Arnett checked his watch. "Now I have another patient, but in Lexie's capable hands, I expect Clint to make a full recovery."

Heavy eyelids. Unresponsive limbs. Still hurting head. But Clint forced himself to claw his way to consciousness. Daylight was streaming through the window, and the first thing he focused on was Lexie. His whole world got better at the sight of her. Why?

"Hi," he muttered.

Her face pinkened. "Hi. You okay?"

Okay how? He closed his eyes again, *trying to piece together what he'd been told.* In the hospital. Bull wreck. Brain injury. Dad was gone. Six months—no, two and a half years ago. If it had been that long, why did it hurt so badly?

Lexie stepped closer and dabbed his cheek with a tissue.

A tear he hadn't realized he'd shed. At least he had Mom and Carly. And Dad's therapist. For the moment. Maybe she made him feel better because he'd seen Dad's progress from working with her.

"Are you hurting anywhere?"

"Just my head." And his brain and heart.

"The nurse can give you something, if you need it," she offered.

"No." He furrowed a brow. "Where are Mom and Carly?"

"Dr. Arnett gave you a sedative so you'd sleep through the night and they hadn't slept in a while, so he sent them home."

"Has it really been two and a half years since Dad died?" Clint asked.

"Yes."

"What else did I miss?"

"We'll get into that later." She let out a world-weary sigh. "Just try to rest. Your brain's on overload."

"Why was I riding a bull if my mom's ranch was in jeopardy two years ago? Is she in financial trouble again?"

"I don't think so," she replied. "From what I understand, you wanted to expand the beefalo business to Fort Worth."

"That's weird. Why would I want a business in Fort Worth?" He closed his eyes, thought hard. Try as he might, he couldn't come up with anything else.

"It's not important right now." She plumped his pillow.

"Will I get better?"

"We're going to do everything we can to recover your memories."

Which didn't answer his question. Why was she dressed in a T-shirt and jeans? "Where's your scrubs?" he asked. "Are you off today?"

"Technically, I don't work here anymore."

Clint frowned in confusion. "You don't?"

"I put in my notice two weeks ago. I'm going to work in the rehab clinic in Bandera. But they don't need me until the end of March."

Yes. Mom had told him she was leaving the hospital. And he'd promptly forgotten. "What about until then?"

She flashed a bright smile. "Meet your new occupational therapist."

"So I'll go to the clinic in Bandera? But you won't be there yet, so how can you be my therapist?"

"Your mom and sister asked me to be your in-home therapist until my new job starts."

His tension eased. She'd helped Dad; surely she could help him. Right?

The door swung open and Dr. Arnett entered. "Good, you're awake. I'll have your release papers ready soon. We're just waiting on the results of one more test, so it may be late this afternoon."

"You mean I can barely walk and I can't remember my two-year-old niece, but you're kicking me out?"

"I wouldn't put it exactly like that." The doctor scanned his monitor. "Most patients can't wait to get the boot from me. Your mom made arrangements to have all the physical therapy equipment you'll need set up at the family ranch. As your OT, Lexie will set up a schedule."

"Wow, I didn't know my insurance was that good."

"You can call if you have any problems and Lexie will bring you to see me in a month, so I can monitor your progress."

Just like that, he was going home. With half a brain. In the hospital he felt sheltered. Shielded from whatever had happened in the last two years. But at home, he'd have to face all of it. His stomach clenched. The unknown was terrifying.

"Don't worry," Lexie said, gently patting his arm. "We'll get you through this."

Her smile reassured his mind a little. No wonder his father had adored her. Dad must have felt exactly like this. Would he follow in his old man's footsteps, losing more and more of his memories? Eventually losing all of himself.

Dear Lord, help me.

What had she gotten herself into? Late-afternoon sunlight streamed through the windows as Lexie helped Clint transfer from the wheelchair to the couch in the Rawlinses' family room, then parked the chair in the corner. She was supposed to be enjoying four weeks of rest and relaxation. Instead, she'd signed up for a month of intensive therapy.

"This is nice." He leaned his head back on a cushion and closed his eyes. "There's no place like home."

Why couldn't she just walk away? she asked herself. And the answer was simple—because she loved Audrey. "I checked out our therapy room. Your equipment is all set up. We'll start in the morning. I'll be here around nine."

"That fast? I just got home."

"No rest for the injured." With him settled, she took the opportunity to look around. The Rawlinses' home was warm and inviting, with a cowhide rug in front of a creamy Austin stone fireplace, overstuffed furniture and massive overhead beams. "Your mom's in the kitchen if you need anything."

"I've put her through the wringer," he murmured, regret echoing in his tone. "I don't know what I was thinking. I don't remember the expansion to Fort Worth idea. Or my decision to compete in the rodeo this year. A year I didn't even know was here. Did I compete last year?"

"I don't know." If he had, not even his sister Carly knew about it. Could he have secretly competed with no one the wiser?

"I honestly don't know why I ended up on that bull's back."

"Well, that's what we're here for. To help you get those answers." She released a breath. "I better take off. I need to unload my car at my parents' and get settled in. You can relax the rest of the day. Tomorrow, we'll begin retrieving your memory and recovering your mobility."

"What if I don't get my memory back?" he asked.

"It's possible. But rare."

"Dad's illness started with memory loss. And it all came from bull wrecks."

Which was why he should have known better. "How many wrecks and concussions did your dad have?"

"I've lost count."

"You've had two."

"That I know of." He groaned. "At the moment, my brain is toast."

"Listen, Clint…" She knelt in front of him. "Part of therapy is a positive attitude. I know it's hard, but you can't dwell on the negatives and have a successful recovery."

He nodded. "Right. I'll work on that."

She patted his hand. And electricity shot through her fingers. Whoa. No touching the cowboy. Since she'd seen him in his hospital bed, she'd been drawn to him. She might get too attached to her patients, but she did not fall for them. Especially some selfish bull rider who'd run off to the rodeo every time he was short on cash.

The doorbell rang and she stood. But before she could respond, the door opened.

Ted entered. And froze when he saw Clint. "Oh, I didn't know you were home yet."

"Who are you?" Clint asked with a frown. "And who do you think you are, barging in my mother's house?"

"Oh, I, um, I rang first." The older gentleman's face went crimson. "I'm, uh, Ted. I didn't think y'all were back from the hospital yet. You must be Clint. And—" His gaze went to Lexie for help.

"I'm Lexie, his therapist." She bit her lip, her mind completely blank on how to help the poor guy out.

"So you're here to do what exactly?" Clint pressed. "Rob us? But robbers usually don't offer their names. Unless Ted isn't really your name."

"Ted goes to our church," Audrey announced, popping up from out of nowhere. "He's here to, um—"

"Feed the cat." Lexie tried to help her out.

"Yes." Audrey smiled. "Thank you, Ted, but as you can see, we're home now."

"I'm glad your son's home, ma'am. I'll just be on my way."

"Mom?"

"Yes, dear."

Clint cast a suspicious glare on Ted's retreating back. "You're allergic to cats."

Chapter Four

Lexie's face heated. She'd made it worse instead of helping. "There was a stray, right, Audrey?"

"Yes," Audrey rushed to say. "As long as it stays outside, it doesn't bother me and I couldn't bear to see the poor thing hungry."

"So if it's outside, why did Ted have to come in the house to feed it?" Skepticism echoed in Clint's tone.

"Because I can't keep the food outside, silly. Every varmint in the county would show up," his mom explained. "Now, speaking of food, I better see what I can come up with for supper. Will you stay and eat with us, Lexie?"

"Thanks for the invite, but I really need to get to my folks' place for the night."

"Of course, tell them hello, and how awesome we think you are."

"We think you're pretty awesome, too," she said, then turned her glance toward Clint. He was watching her with his intense green eyes. Thoughts unreadable. Her face got hotter. "See you tomorrow, bright and early. Be ready to get to work." With a wave goodbye to Audrey, she hurried out the door and to her car.

Backing out with her possessions piled to the ceiling in the back seat was no small feat. Since her apartment had been furnished, thankfully all she had to move was clothing, photos, decor items and keepsakes. Once on the familiar highway, she allowed her mind to roam.

Clint was a tough nut to crack. Would he ever let her in enough to help him? He'd been a bit more open with her at the hospital when they'd been alone. His dad had been the same. Stoic and invincible as long as his family was around. But alone in their therapy sessions, he'd let his guard down and his vulnerabilities had shown. Hopefully, Clint would be the same.

Her parents' house came into view, promptly turning her all misty-eyed. She'd wanted to move home for so long, and finally, it was happening. By the time she turned into the drive and parked, she couldn't see a thing. She wondered if they were home from her best friend's ranch, where they both worked.

She swiped at her eyes. A tall, lean figure stood near the barn, looking her way. He adjusted his hat and sauntered in her direction. Daddy's familiar, long stride put a lump in her throat. As he neared the house, Mama stepped out on the porch with a dish towel clutched in one hand. Her other hand went to her heart. Even though it had only been a few months since Christmas, when Lexie had last visited, her vision blurred even more as she climbed out of her car and hurried toward the porch.

"Welcome home." Mama dabbed tears with the dish towel, then drew her into a hug.

Daddy engulfed them both. "So glad you're home, pudding." A mixture of sweat, Stetson cologne, hay, horse and a touch of saddle leather filled her senses. If you looked up "real cowboy" in the dictionary, you'd likely find a picture of her dad, Denny Parker—ranch foreman extraordinaire.

"Me, too."

"You make the drive okay?" Daddy cleared his throat,

the only indication of his emotion, and pulled away to open the screen door for them.

"Just fine."

"I made chicken and dressing, your favorite."

"You didn't have to do that, Mama." She caught a whiff of sage and other spices as she stepped inside. "But I'm so glad you did."

The porch door clapped shut behind Daddy. The old farmhouse had been remodeled and updated through the years. Except for the screen door. Because Mama liked the sound of it. Lexie did, too.

"I'm so glad I don't live in San Antonio anymore." She closed her eyes, letting the peaceful small farm noises wash over her. The constant traffic and hustle of the city had never grown on her.

From the time she'd gotten her degree and her job at the hospital, her goal had been to move home and get her own place. And with her temporary job with the Rawlins family, she'd be able to afford to rent or maybe even buy a house sooner than she'd expected.

Now to tell Mama and Daddy about the month off she no longer had.

"I hope you're hungry." Mama led the way to the kitchen, where the table was already set with sweet potatoes and broccoli cheese casserole accompanying the main dish.

"Always, for your cooking. It looks like Thanksgiving."

"We're thankful to have our girl home." Daddy filled three glasses with ice, poured sweet tea and set them in their regular spots at one end of the long farmhouse table.

"It looks and smells wonderful. But I hate that you went to so much trouble after cooking breakfast and lunch for a bunch of hungry hands at the ranch."

"Larae insisted I leave early today since you were coming." Mama took her seat as Lexie and Daddy settled in theirs. "I don't have many talents, so I enjoy sharing the one I have."

"That's so not true." The house was a testimony to Mama's many talents. From the handmade curtain toppers and bedspreads Mama sewed in her spare time to the touches of cozy farm decor spread throughout the house. "I can't wait to pick fabric for curtains once I get my own place."

"Look through my stash first," Mama said with a laugh. "I've got yards and yards. Some I bought just because I liked it and I've even got some I bought with future grandchildren in mind."

"Way in the future." Lexie rolled her eyes at the subtle hint.

"Don't you be in a hurry to move out," Daddy said, scooping heaping helpings on his plate, then smaller portions for Lexie and Mama. "We just got you home."

With the food served, they clasped hands. "Dear Lord—" Daddy cleared his throat "—we do thank You for this food. For bringing our girl home. For safe travels and for the mountain of blessings You give us daily. In Jesus's precious name, amen."

Mama squeezed her hand before turning loose. "I wish I could take some time off before your new job starts. But the ranch is really busy. Maybe you can come to work with me, be my sous-chef."

Lexie savored the crumbly, melt-in-your-mouth cornbread dressing. "About that, I sort of took a temporary job that starts tomorrow."

"You didn't." Mama sighed. "You've been burning your candle at both ends since you went off to college. If you don't take a break, you'll burn yourself out."

"I'm fine, Mama. And you're one to talk! When's the last time you took time off?"

"She's got you there, Stella. Like mother, like daughter." Daddy chuckled. "What kind of job?"

"Do y'all remember me working with Levi Rawlins?"

"Sure do," Daddy said, taking a swig of his tea. "He was a good neighbor. Moved to Medina after you went off to school. It was a crying shame when he got sick."

"But Lexie helped him." Mama forked a slice of candied sweet potato. "I run into Audrey often and she never fails to mention how our girl made Levi's last days more functional and enjoyable."

"Didn't I hear her boy had a bull wreck recently?" Daddy frowned, obviously trying to pull up details. "Seems like somebody mentioned him on the prayer list Sunday."

Lexie nodded. "Audrey asked me to work with him at their ranch here in Medina. I couldn't say no."

"Of course you couldn't," Mama murmured, patting her arm. "That's good. Poor Audrey's been through the wringer. She needs you. And there's no sense in you rattling around here all day with nothing to do while we're working. We'll still have some time in the evenings, right? You won't work ridiculous hours."

"I thought they needed some family time to get him settled tonight. I'm planning to work nine to five, but it depends on how he handles the frustration of his condition and how quickly he progresses."

"Our little Florence Nightingale to the rescue," Daddy said proudly. "That boy will be good as new before you know it."

Lexie sure hoped so. Despite Clint's calm demeanor with his family, she'd seen the fear in his eyes when they'd been alone in his hospital room. The same fear she'd seen in his dad's gaze almost three years before.

Still in the fifties, but the sun was supposed to come out and warm things up by noon. Before Lexie could press the Rawlinses' bell, the door opened.

Carly greeted her with a frown, then ushered her inside. "Mom's in the shower. But beware. He's a bear this morning."

"Is it normal for him to be grumpy?" Or was he exhibiting personality changes?

"When things aren't going his way, he gets really frustrated. It started with supper last night. He had a hard time feeding himself, but he wouldn't let me or Mom help. He retreated to his room to eat by himself and it went downhill from there."

"You should have called me."

"We calmed him down, then looked at photo albums from the last two years, like Dr. Arnett recommended."

"Good."

"But his mood isn't any better this morning, and he insisted on eating breakfast alone in the therapy room."

"There you are." Clint rolled up behind Carly. "Let's get this party started." His grim tone didn't match his words.

"Lead the way."

He painstakingly backed his chair up with awkward hands that obviously didn't quite do what his brain told them to.

"Here, let me help." Carly rolled him toward the bedroom Ted had converted into a therapy room. Cleared of furniture, the room was graced only by a set of parallel bars, a triangular-shaped trapeze support, a treadmill and a balance ball, along with a small table and chairs. But family pictures lined the taupe walls, keeping it from being too austere. A thoughtful touch to encourage Clint. Audrey's doing or had the room always held the collection?

"I can do it," Clint growled.

"I know you can, but it won't kill you to let me help," Carly huffed.

Scrambled eggs dotted the floor along with link sausages scattered about.

"Just a little accident." Clint's jaw tensed. The dark stubble did nothing to hide the chiseled lines of his handsome face.

"No worries. I'll get a dustpan and bring a new plate," Carly told him before scurrying out of the room.

"I ate enough. I'm fine."

"Breakfast is the most important meal of the day." Lexie waggled her eyebrows at him, trying to lighten things up. "Especially if you plan to work hard. And I *will* put you through your paces."

"Bring it." The intensity in his eyes turned steely.

"All right, hotshot, take it easy. We'll see what you got. As soon as you get some food in your stomach."

Carly returned with a fresh plate.

"I got this." Lexie took it and the broom from her. "Thanks. Can you shut the door behind you?"

Carly looked from her to Clint. "I gotta get to work anyway. Aye, aye, Sarge." She saluted, clicked her heels and left them alone.

Lexie set the plate on the bistro-style table she'd asked Ted to set up in the room. "Eat up while I tidy up a bit."

"I can't." Clint spewed out a sigh. "That's how the first plate's contents ended up in the floor. My hands work worse than a toddler's."

"Where did you try to eat? At the table?"

"No."

"Try the table. That way you won't have to balance your plate and your fork."

"Makes sense." He hesitated. "Want to give me a hand? It'll take me three days to get over there."

"You can do it. Chop-chop." She lightly clapped her hands.

He rolled his eyes and slowly turned his chair toward the table while she swept up the eggs and sausage, then got a wet washcloth and towel from the adjoining bathroom to wipe up the greasy spots on the hardwood floor.

By the time she finished her cleanup, he'd made it to the table and was pushing a bite of egg across his plate.

"Here." She sat beside him, repositioned the fork in his fingers with tines up. "Now concentrate."

He stabbed at the egg, but missed by a good inch. "You can take over for me anytime. It bugs the life out of me when Mom or Carly try to do things for me. But I guess I figure you've seen folks in worse shape than me."

"Try again. If I do things for you, you'll never get to where you can do it yourself."

"This is so embarrassing." He managed to stab the egg but missed his mouth by an inch. Red splotches bathed his face.

"You can do it."

He dragged the egg across his cheek, found his mouth.

"Open sesame."

"You're enjoying this." He popped the bite in and chewed.

"Yes, when you make progress, I enjoy it." Why was it always so hard for the self-sufficient male to admit weakness? "Let's get some things straight," she told him firmly. "Your brain is struggling to tell your fingers what to do. You're recovering from a head injury. There's no reason to be embarrassed about what you can and can't do. Your family understands and they love and support you. No one cares if you miss your mouth, spill anything or make a mess."

"I know." He'd managed to stab a sausage link and hit his cheek again. "But if it's all the same to you, I'd like to keep meals in here until I get better at it." He slid the sausage to his mouth, then bit the end of it off.

"That's why I put the table in here."

"Thanks." He eyed her scrubs, black dotted with cartoon cats. "So you're a cat person?"

"Yes. And thoroughly enjoying being able to wear whatever scrubs I want. A lot of hospitals and clinics choose a certain solid color for each profession. OTs wore burgundy. Period. I hate wearing the same thing every day. I feel like people think I never do laundry."

"You smell too good for them to think that."

Her gaze met his. "Thanks." Cheeks warming, she swallowed the knot his compliment put in her throat.

"Do you have a cat?"

"No, my apartment didn't allow pets. But I'm hoping to find a pet-friendly rental house here."

"You hungry?"

"No. My mom made a big breakfast this morning."

"Your folks are great. Your mom sent lots of meals and your dad helped with keeping the yard mowed when Dad was sick." His tone tightened at the mention of his dad, as if he needed to rein in his emotions. "I can't believe we never met, with them living right down the road and going to the same church."

"I lived and worked in San Antonio for the last eight and a half years. And didn't get to come home for visits as much as I would've liked. I've mostly been home for holidays and birthdays."

"I still can't believe it's been two and a half years since Dad..." His eyes dimmed. "Even though Mom and Carly showed me photo albums. Pictures spanning two years I don't remember. How can I not remember my own niece?"

"The brain is a magnificent mystery."

"I need to remember," he muttered, raking a bite of egg off his plate.

"Don't worry. Or stress about it. The more relaxed you are, the more progress we'll make." She stood, strode over to the closet. "Now finish eating, while I get our therapy tools ready. And concentrate on what you're doing."

"Anybody ever tell you you're bossy?" He gave her a lopsided grin.

"I've learned I have to be, when dealing with the fully grown, stubborn male species." She pulled the balance ball and a large mat out to the center of the room. Then set a deck of cards, a board game and a jigsaw puzzle on the table. "But I prefer the term *take-charge*."

"What's all that?"

"Therapy."

"I'm supposed to play games?" Skepticism dripped from his words.

"They each require small motor skills and reasoning, which is what we need to retrain your brain to do."

"But I thought I'd walk parallel bars or the treadmill."

"You don't need me for the parallel bars," she informed him. "The ball will help your balance and we'll try the treadmill later. Baby steps and patience will get you where you want to be. Trust me."

"I saw what you did for my dad, so that I can do." He pushed his plate away. "Between what I managed to eat from the first plate, plus this one, I'm about to pop."

Lexie scanned his plate. One sausage and a dab of egg left. Nothing on the table. Her gaze narrowed on him. "You cleaned up while I wasn't looking, didn't you?"

Clint ducked his head. "Yes, but I did better. This was all that ended up on the table."

"What do you think was the difference in the first plate and the second plate?"

Concentration formed creases across his forehead. He was really quite handsome. And probably normally pretty easygoing and kind, like his parents. How had he stayed single? She shook the thought away. He was a patient and she had no business thinking about his looks or personality traits.

"My plate was on the table. You told me I could do it. To stay relaxed and focus. So I did."

"Excellent. We've made progress here already. You spilled less, you did what I told you to, and you reasoned out why it worked."

"Baby steps," he echoed.

"You need to use your napkin."

"Of course, since I missed my mouth with every bite." He reached for the napkin, managed to grip it with clumsy fingers and swiped for his mouth.

But ended up getting only his cheek.

"Here, let me help." She placed her hand over his, helped him move the napkin to his mouth. Her fingers tingled as she met his gaze, and she jerked her hand away. "That's better. Okay, let's get you out of that chair."

"Please." The vulnerability in his voice tugged at her.

She locked the wheels. "You can use the chair, table and me for support."

Using mostly the table and chair, he pushed up. Once standing, he held on to her arm as she walked him toward the balance ball. His feet made awkward, uncoordinated movements, slapping heavily against the floor. Every few steps, he swayed a bit. But at least he stepped onto the mat she'd put down in case of falls, without catching his toe on it.

"Why won't my feet obey?" he grumbled.

"Don't worry, you're doing fine. Now, whatever you do, don't just plop down on the ball. It will throw you just like that bull did. Just ease down onto it."

"I'm not sure I can balance enough to do that and I don't think you're big enough to support me while I do it."

"That's where this comes in." She gestured to the trapeze support hanging from the ceiling above the ball.

"Grab it, and use your arm strength to ease down and stay balanced."

He grabbed the bar, took a deep breath and lowered himself. Slow and precise, he sank onto the ball.

"You don't have to let go today if you don't think you're ready."

"I was ready yesterday." He let go of the bar, rocked to the right, then the left, and managed to right himself. But then he swayed left again.

Lexie grabbed his shoulders, trying to steady him. But his weight was too much. He flipped off the ball, taking her with him. They landed on the mat, him on his back, her sprawled sideways beside him.

"You okay?" She rose up.

He covered his face with both hands, his shoulders shaking.

Watching a full-grown man cry, even silently, always did her in. "I'm sorry. I should have made you hang on to the bar. Are you hurt?"

"I'm fine." He moved his hands. Laughing, not crying. "That was fun. Can we do it again?"

"No." She lay down on her back, blowing out a relieved sigh. Tension eased as his deep laughter continued.

A knock sounded at the door and it opened as Audrey stepped in. "Oh dear, is everything okay?"

"I'm fine, Mom. The balance ball bucked me off." He roared with laughter. "I used to ride bulls and now I can't even ride a hoppity-hop without taking my therapist out, too."

Audrey looked worried, but Clint's amusement proved contagious. She chuckled. "Okay, then, I'll leave you two to it." The door shut.

"I forgot about hoppity-hops." She couldn't stay serious any longer and joined in his laughter. Until she didn't hear him anymore and looked over at him.

Tears trickled into the dark hair at his temple. But not from laughter.

She looked away, closed her eyes and prayed silently for his comfort and peace.

He heaved a big breath, swiped at his eyes and said, "Okay, pity party over. But I'm not sure if I can get up."

"Roll onto your side."

He followed her instructions.

"Now use your hands and arms to push your upper body up first." She helped him position correctly and leveraged her weight against him for support. "Great. Put your top knee forward, then get on your hands and knees. Now crawl over to the chair at the table and slowly push up from the seat of it."

"Oh, that's humiliating." His tone dripped with sarcasm.

"There will be times I'm not here and you'll need to get from one place to the other," she reminded him. "Would you rather have to call your mom every time?"

With a sigh, he crawled over to the chair and did as she directed.

"Don't ever try to pull up on the back of the chair or on the table, since they might tip over." She helped him ease into the chair. "How about we play cards?"

"Just give me a minute, then I'll go for another ride."

"Only if you hold on to the trapeze bar. Period."

"We'll see." He grinned, but it didn't reach his eyes. "For the record, I don't cry."

"What happens in the therapy room stays in the therapy room," she said gently. "But for the record, the part of your brain you injured controls emotion. And you've been through a lot." His dad's death was still fresh for him, and he'd lost two years of his life, including the birth of a new niece. "You're entitled to a good pity party crying binge."

"No, thank you. I think I'm ready to ride the ball again."

"Once you get stronger and your balance improves, you

can push yourself. But for now, let's take it slow and easy. I'll only allow you to try the ball again if you promise to hold on to the trapeze."

"Yes, Sarge." He made an awkward salute.

But despite his tears earlier, Lexie felt encouraged. His determination would drive him to recovery. And his mood had been more upbeat than she'd expected. All she had to do was make sure he didn't drive himself into the ground.

Chapter Five

Day two of therapy was two thirds over and lunch had been a mess. With more beans on the table than in Clint's growling stomach. But Lexie insisted he was doing great. Did she only say that because it was her job? He certainly didn't feel great. He felt uncoordinated, incapable, disjointed, inept.

Powerless.

Was this how Dad had felt? Would he gradually get worse and worse like his father had?

Today's accomplishment: he'd learned Lexie was equally a dog person, since she'd shown up wearing scrubs scattered with different breeds.

And she was very patient and good at sensing when he needed a break. They'd spent the bulk of the afternoon with him seated at the kitchen table between her and Mom, poring over photo albums.

"This was when Charlee was born. That little darling sure loves her Uncle Clint." He tried to focus on the photo Mom was showing him. The hairless, toothless infant looked much like Cooper had as a newborn. Brain injury or no, how could he have forgotten his niece's birth?

"Hey, everybody." Carly hurried in.

"I didn't even hear the door," Mom said, standing up. "Want supper?"

"No, I can't stay long. Just wanted to see how your therapy's going."

"I'm pleased with the progress Clint made today." Lexie smiled.

"Wow, progress on the second day," Carly remarked, kissing his cheek. "Gotta go. But I'll be able to come over tomorrow night and spend some time with my little bro. So do me a favor, Lexie, don't work him too hard."

"I have a feeling I'll be trying to put his brakes on through the entire month."

"Uncle Clint." A small voice came from the hallway as a young boy stepped into sight.

"Cooper!" Carly gasped. "I told you to stay in the car."

Cooper? A foot taller than Clint remembered. And two years older. His towhead gone. Darker hair with a few sun-lightened streaks. How could this be?

"But I wanted to see Uncle Clint."

"Where's your sister?" Carly demanded, starting for the door.

"I brought her in with me." Cooper stepped aside to reveal a toddler standing behind him.

"Cooper, please go to the car." Carly scooped up her daughter. "I'll see you tomorrow night, Clint."

Seeing grown-up Cooper in pictures and grown-up Cooper *in person* were two entirely different things. And Charlee, out of the womb and walking, blew his mind.

"No." The word ripped from Clint. "Don't go."

"See, Uncle Clint wants to see me, too," Cooper said, darting toward him. "Don't you?" The youngster frowned. "Or do you even remember me?"

"I do remember." Clint reached for him. "A younger version of you."

Cooper plowed into him. Good thing he was sitting down.

"Careful, Cooper. Remember I told you Uncle Clint hurt his head. He gets off balance easy, so you can't be rough with him."

"It's okay since I was sitting." His arms came around his nephew. He may be taller and older, but this felt the same. Smelled the same. Sweat and dirt, with a hint of shampoo, no longer baby scented.

"I'm glad you're okay, Uncle Clint."

"Me, too."

The toddler ran over to him and clambered up in his lap. "Uncle Squint."

He chuckled at the mispronunciation.

Carly grinned. "That's what she's always called you."

"I like it." Charlee. The last time he'd seen her in person, she was still in Carly's stomach. It made his head hurt. And his heart.

Cooper pulled away from him, staring with rounded eyes. "Why are you crying, Uncle Clint?"

"Remember I told you, he might be weird." Carly winced, obviously regretting her choice of words.

Clint chuckled again. Weird and surreal, that fit.

"But I've never seen Uncle Clint cry. Ever. Not even when Grandpa died."

That stole the breath out of his lungs. But at least he remembered. He'd cried all right. Just not in front of anyone.

"I think we should go," Carly hedged.

"No. Please. Don't take them," he rasped, managing a smile. "I'm crying because I missed y'all." Missed two years to be exact. "And I'm happy to see you again." Even though he'd never seen Charlee. That he could remember anyway.

"Lexie, what do you think?" Carly looked to her for confirmation.

"I think it's a great idea for Clint to spend time with people who love him."

"Okay. I guess we've got a few hours before Bible study tonight," his sister said.

Clint hadn't even realized it was Wednesday. Would he ever get to the point where he could go to church? Keep a schedule?

"Just what the doctor ordered." He buried his nose in Charlee's fine downy hair. Baby shampoo and powder filled his senses. Worry-free innocence soothed his troubled soul.

"How come you're in a wheelchair, Uncle Clint?" Cooper piped up.

"Your uncle Clint hurt the part of his brain that controls his balance, so it's hard for him to stand and walk right now." Lexie explained, making it sound like it was no big deal. "But we're working on it, so he'll be on his feet and steady like before."

"What else is weird about him?"

"Cooper, not so many questions, bud," Carly cautioned.

"He's just being Cooper. Always full of questions." At least his nephew hadn't changed. He set his hand on his nephew's head to ruffle his hair, but his hand just flopped. "My hands have a hard time understanding what my brain wants. That makes precise movements hard for me."

"So we can't build LEGO houses?"

"Actually, that would be great therapy." Lexie stood and hurried to their therapy room.

"Who's she?" Cooper whispered.

"My therapist. She's helping me remember how to stand and walk and work my hands."

"Cool. She seems nice. And pretty. Do you think she's pretty, Uncle Clint?"

He'd definitely noticed her thick cascade of midnight hair with equally dark, enigmatic eyes and flawless skin. "Lexie is very pretty."

"Ahem." Carly cleared her throat, drawing Clint's attention.

Lexie stood just behind his sister with a big yellow box shaped like one huge LEGO brick. The splash of pink across her cheeks gave tangible evidence she'd heard what he said.

His face flushed. "But more important, she's a really good therapist." And that was all he needed to see her as. If he was following his dad's mental path, he couldn't possibly entertain anything else.

"I'll get out of your hair for the night," she said, setting the box on the table. "Call me if you run into any problems." With a wave, she scurried for the front door.

Running for her life. From a guy with no future. Did she know something about his prognosis that he didn't?

No. No. No. Lexie shook her head.

She could not be attracted to Clint, even if he thought she was pretty. She could not get tingling fingers every time she touched him during therapy. She could not think about how handsome he was while helping him with a task.

She turned into Larae's drive. Her friend had texted her throughout the day, begging her to stop by on the way home. Until Lexie agreed, insisting she couldn't stay long or eat since Mama would have supper ready soon and they had church to attend tonight.

The long drive ended at the cedar-sided ranch house with the long porch and inviting swing. Exactly the same as when she'd been a kid. Comforting. She killed the engine and crawled out of her cocoon. Now that she wouldn't be driving back and forth from the city for visits, maybe she'd invest in something bigger.

At the second step, the door swung open. "I'm so happy you're home!" Larae exclaimed, wrapping her up in a hug.

Even though it had only been a few months since they'd seen each other.

"Me, too."

"Come on in. It's chilly out here." Rance Shepherd ushered them inside.

Larae's husband.

And even though Lexie had attended the grand opening of Larae's indoor rodeo last summer, witnessed the proposal and been in the wedding the very next day, she still couldn't get used to them being together.

"Speaking of chili, I told your mom we should have supper here. Of course I offered to cook, but she insisted on making us a pot." Larae followed her in.

"That sounds nice." The pastel-flowered couch stood the test of time in the fancy living room and always brought back memories of her friend's very genteel Southern mom.

"Lexie!" Jayda bolted down the stairs in the foyer and blasted into her.

"Hey, buttercup," Lexie murmured, picking her up and swinging her around. "You've grown. I may not be able to do this much longer."

"I grew a whole inch since the wedding."

"I can tell." She set Jayda down, pressed a kiss on her head.

"Me and Daddy are gonna go finish the cake we made, so you and Mama can talk. He's trying to win you over."

Lexie snickered, looking up at Rance. "You don't have to win me over. As long as these two are happy, so am I."

"Come on, baby girl, since you outed me, we best git to it." Rance kissed Larae's cheek and steered Jayda to the kitchen.

Larae watched them go with a dreamy look on her face.

"Is he really for real?"

"Completely," Larae replied, clasping a hand to her heart.

"I'm glad. It's good to see you happy." Over the years Larae had transformed from a heartbroken single mom, to career woman, to a wife and mom with a happily-ever-after. Made Lexie wish for one of those for herself.

"So how was your day?" Larae plopped on her mom's vintage couch and patted the pastel floral cushion.

"Better than I expected," Lexie said, settling down beside her friend. "I was afraid he'd be frustrated from the get-go, but we made some progress today and his frame of mind was encouraging." And he thought she was pretty.

"What was that?"

"What?" she asked.

"Something just passed across your face, like delight, and then wariness."

"I overheard him tell his nephew he thinks I'm pretty." Lexie rolled her eyes.

"Well, it certainly won't be the first time a patient has fallen for you. It's part of the job. Kind of like the doctor-patient thing. In a sense you save their lives." Larae swatted her thigh. "And just look at you. You're a living doll. No wonder they get smitten. How old is he?"

Her face heated. "Twenty-eight." *But he only remembers up to twenty-six.*

"Oh, I see." Larae chuckled. "He's cute. And single. It's a two-way street, isn't it?"

"But it can't be," Lexie moaned, burying her face into her hands.

"Why not?"

"He's my patient." She peeked out from between her fingers.

"So?" Larae pulled her hands away. "Once you get him all recovered, he won't be."

"You're not helping."

"I'm *trying* to," her friend huffed. "You've been so focused on your career your love life has died on the vine."

"You're one to talk. You were in the same boat until last year, when you moved back home and ran into Rance again."

"And just look at me now." Larae's smile turned sappy. "I didn't know life could be so good. I mean—I was happy being Jayda's mom and I loved my job at the rodeo in Fort Worth. But being married to Rance, completing our family with Jayda, it's pure bliss."

"I can tell."

"So back to your cute patient," Larae said, redirecting Lexie to the matter at hand. "Once he's recovered, you should date him. How long's it been since you were on a date?"

She actually couldn't remember. "That's a terrible idea! It's unethical for me to date my patient. And besides that, he rides bulls. I've had way too many bull wreck patients, so I know what those monsters can do. His father died because of a bull and Clint promised his family he'd stop, but he didn't."

She remembered suddenly that Larae ran a rodeo. "No offense, but not only is he a rodeo junkie, he lies. And to top everything off, I can't trust his emotions because he has a traumatic brain injury. I *so* can *not* be attracted to him."

"But you already are," Larae said, shooting her a knowing smile.

"I'm such a failure." She covered her face with her hands again.

"Stop it."

"I've never been attracted to a patient. Never."

"So what will you do about that?" Larae asked.

"I'll ignore it. Do my job. And never see him again."

It was only a month. She could resist Clint's tall, dark and vulnerable charms for a month, minus the half a week she already had under her belt. Couldn't she?

* * *

Mom was acting weird this morning. She'd been dusting shelves that didn't need dusting when Clint had gotten up. Seemed nervous and agitated as she cooked breakfast. Even with the smell of bacon, the scent of lemon cleaner hung in the air, almost enough to make him sneeze. Was she working up the nerve to blast him for competing in the rodeo after he'd promised not to? He'd expected her to be livid. Instead, she'd just been worried.

Why had he competed? The ranch was in the black. It had been two years since it was in trouble. Two years of memories he couldn't come up with, no matter how long he sat here at the kitchen table browsing through pictures.

He flipped the page. Pictures of Cooper and newborn Charlee. He ran his fingertips over the images as if he could recapture the day by touching it. It had been good to see them last night. Even if it did boggle his brain. Even more than it was already boggled.

"You sure you're not hungry? You need to eat something before Lexie puts you through your paces."

"I'm fine."

"I need to tell you something." Mom set her dustrag down on an end table.

"Okay." Here we go.

"Dr. Arnett said we should break the news gently, let you get settled in. You did so well yesterday and I hate keeping things from you."

This wasn't about the rodeo. A sense of dread coiled in his stomach. "What is it?"

"I know that to you it doesn't seem like it's been two and a half years since we lost your daddy. But is has been. A painfully long time."

"What haven't you told me?"

Mom closed her eyes. "I'm engaged."

He sucked in a breath as if she'd kicked him in the gut.

"I'm sorry. Maybe this is too soon to tell you." She clasped his hand. "Ted won't come around. Not until you get better. But I was so afraid one of the kids would let it slip last night. And I wanted you to hear it from me."

Ted? "The cat guy?"

"Yes."

"There was no stray cat, was there?"

"No. Lexie pulled that out of thin air. She was just trying to help me cover until you were more settled in. Of course she didn't know I'm allergic." Mom rambled when she was nervous.

He searched his memory for scraps of Ted. Nothing. Apart from the other day when he'd first gotten home. "Do I like this Ted guy?"

"I think so. You've been very supportive. You even offered to walk me down the aisle."

"He's good to you?" he asked.

"Yes." She squeezed his hand, her voice shaking with emotion "I'll always love your father, Clint. Ted doesn't change that. In fact, I never thought I'd even date anyone. I thought I'd just remain a widow for the rest of my days. But I was so very lonely until Ted moved to the area six months ago. We met at church."

"Well, if you're gonna meet someone, that's a good place." He tried to sound normal, like he was okay with this. In his mind, Dad had died six months ago. In reality, Mom hadn't met Ted until Dad had been gone for two years. He had to reconcile that in his head. "You've only known him six months and you're already engaged? He's not some gold digger who found a pretty lady with a solvent ranch, is he?"

Mom chuckled. "Definitely not. Do you remember hearing of Townsend Gas & Oil?"

"They started drilling for natural gas in the area back

when Dad was sick. He was hoping they'd drill on our property."

"That's right. Well, Ted Townsend owns the company."

"And he's not after your mineral rights?" he prodded.

"Trust me, Ted doesn't need my piddly hundred acres. I offered to sign a prenup, but he wouldn't hear of it."

"Does he have kids?"

"No. His wife was a diabetic, so they agreed not to have kids. For her health and to avoid passing the disease on." Mom sighed. "She went into a renal failure and died a few months after your father."

A rich widower with no kids. No baggage. Sounded too good to be true.

"You okay?" she whispered, hugging him tight.

"Just trying to digest." His heart hurt.

She let go, patted his cheek.

"Is there anything else I don't know?"

"Nothing of importance." Her gaze locked on his.

"I'm exhausted. I think I'll go back to bed."

She frowned. "But you haven't eaten yet and Lexie will be here soon."

"Just tell her I'm sleeping in." He rolled himself down the hall toward his room.

Mom was engaged.

That made the fact that Dad had been gone for two and a half years painfully real.

Chapter Six

Lexie had barely pulled in the drive when Audrey came rushing out of the house. She jumped out of her car and hurried to meet her.

"What's wrong?"

"I'm so glad you're here. I was so worried Cooper or Charlee would spill the beans about Ted, so I decided to tell Clint about him this morning."

"How did he react?" Lexie asked.

"He went back to bed, said to tell you he's sleeping in."

"How long ago?"

Audrey checked her watch. "Maybe thirty minutes. I shouldn't have told him. But he had such a good day yesterday and he handled seeing the kids so well. I hate keeping secrets from him and I wanted to make sure he heard it from me." She did a facepalm. "Oh, what have I done?"

"He needed to know. And better this way than someone accidentally letting it slip. I'm sure he'll be fine." Maybe this would distract them both from their mutual attraction.

Audrey ushered her inside.

"Where's his room?"

"Second one on the left."

Lexie strode down the hall, rapped her knuckles on the closed door. "Rise and shine, lazybones."

"I'm tired."

"No rest for the weary," she told him.

"I thought you said I needed rest."

"You've had it. Now time's a-wasting. Do you want out of that chair? Or not?"

Movement sounded inside.

"Do you need help?"

"No. I've got it."

"Great. See you in the therapy room. Chop-chop." She clapped her hands, then shot Audrey a grin as she stepped back into the kitchen. "Sometimes I have to be firm. But he wants out of his chair, so that's a good sign."

"I hope so," Audrey murmured, setting a plate of eggs, sausage and biscuits on the table. "I warmed his plate in the microwave. I think while you're working with him today—" she lowered her voice "—I'll slip out and see Ted."

"Good idea. I'm sure he'll make you feel better."

"I feel like a teenager sneaking around behind my parents' back," Audrey admitted.

"Hopefully, it won't be long before things can get back to normal."

The bedroom door opened and Clint rolled into the kitchen. "Let's go, Sarge."

"I'm going to run errands. Lexie won't let you get to work until you eat." Audrey kissed him on the temple. "Eat your breakfast at the table."

"Thanks, Mom."

"Are you hungry, Lexie?"

"No, Mama made me eat before I left."

"I figured Stella wouldn't let you leave with an empty stomach. I'll be back in time to cook lunch." Audrey scrutinized Clint.

"Don't worry, Mom. I'm okay."

Audrey blew out a big breath, squeezed his shoulder and hurried out.

Clint scanned her pink scrubs, dotted with burgundy roses. “You’re looking rosy today.”

“So are you okay, really?” she pressed.

“In my mind, my dad died six months ago and my mom is engaged to a guy she met six months ago.”

“But you know that’s not the case?”

“Yes,” he answered quietly. “But knowing it and experiencing it are two different things. So this Ted guy, have you met him?”

“At the hospital when you were in the ER.”

“He was there?”

“He was very worried about you. And your mom.” She pushed his plate closer to him. “Eat up before it gets cold.”

The next several minutes were filled with Clint’s fork scraping on his plate, hitting his cheek with each bite he took before sliding it into his mouth.

“Do you have to watch every jerky movement I make?”

“Watching your movements helps me determine how to help you,” she informed him. “Even though you’re still hitting your cheek, I think you’re closer than yesterday and you haven’t raked any food off your plate.”

“I guess that’s something to be thankful for.” He managed to swipe at his cheek and mouth with a napkin. “So you’ve seen him with my mom?”

“He’s crazy about her. At the hospital, he was very comforting and encouraging. She was on an emotional roller coaster, until he arrived. He steadied her, gave her strength.”

“He just seems too perfect. Loaded, no kids.”

“Maybe God figured your mom had struggled enough financially since she lost your dad and she didn’t need any more kids to keep her up at night since she already has you,” she murmured.

His gaze narrowed.

"Just saying." She grinned.

"So you really think he's good for her?"

"I do. And for you. He paid the rental tab for all of your rehab equipment and he's paying my salary."

He let out a long whistle. "I thought it was insurance money."

"That only takes care of your hospital bill and rehab if you'd stayed there. But your mom wanted you home and Ted made it happen."

A muscle ticked in his jaw. "So he's either trying to buy her affection or he wants her to be happy."

"From what I've seen, he doesn't need to buy her love." *God, please give me the words.* "I know it's hard to think of your mom with someone else. I loved Levi. But he's been gone for a lot longer than you remember. Ted's a great guy and they love each other."

He swallowed hard. "Why did we never meet when you were working with Dad?"

"I worked with him during the day."

"While I worked the ranch and only came at night."

Remembering her favorite patient always made her smile. "He talked about you a lot. About all of your family while we played chess, his favorite game, and he always beat me." She'd had to learn the game in order to be able to play with him at all.

"He always beat me, too. Until near the end," he said gruffly, his eyes glossing over. "But even then, he still wanted to play."

Memories played through her mind. "He was very proud of you moving back home when he got sick. For stepping up and helping with the ranch. And he was impressed that you had the idea of taking it to new places with beefalo."

"He loved hearing all the ranch news, seeing pictures

of the stock I'd bought and sold. Going over the numbers for profit and loss."

"It kept him feeling involved," she confided. "I think it kept his mind sharp for longer than it would have been, too."

"Really?"

"Definitely, along with the chess games. It's not a game for sissies."

He met her gaze. "You said you loved him."

"He was my favorite patient."

Clint's voice was thick. "He was a great dad."

"And you were a great son to him."

He blinked, swiping his napkin across his eyes with pretty good aim. "Let's go put Ted's equipment to good use. I want out of this chair. Especially if I'm supposed to walk my mom down the aisle anytime soon."

"Challenge accepted." She stood, dumped his last bite of egg in the trash and stuck the plate in the dishwasher.

Had they just bonded? Not good. Not good at all.

She had to get this under control if she was going to be spending all day, every day with Clint. No bonding, no getting personally involved with him, and definitely no falling for the bunged-up cowboy.

Yesterday, after the Ted reveal, Clint had been unable to focus on therapy. Despite having his own personal drill sergeant. Thankfully, today was going better. He swayed from side to side on the balance ball, then managed to steady himself.

"Very good." Lexie pointed a finger at him. "But no letting go of the bar just yet."

"I'm not."

"But you were thinking about it."

Clint shrugged. "Guilty as charged."

"How about the parallel bars now?"

"Really?" he asked.

"Yes, it's about time. Want to use your chair or the walker to get there?"

"Neither." The walker made him feel as old and useful as the chair did. "And the chair isn't mine."

"Feeling confident today, are we?" She smirked. "Okay, use the ladder bar to pull up with. Just don't let go and fall on me."

"Watch this." Though she was around five-seven and athletic, he had a good six inches on her and probably outweighed her by sixty to eighty pounds at least. He pulled himself up. Not pretty or graceful by any means. But he'd done it on his own thanks to hoisting hay bales since his teenage years.

"Very good." She offered him her elbow.

He slid his hand into the crook of her arm, caught a whiff of coconut. Long, dark waves brushed his bicep as she walked him toward the parallel bars. Beautiful, tough, but caring. It was a wonder all her patients didn't fall for her. Especially in her cute yellow scrubs speckled with watermelon slices.

But he couldn't go there. Not with half a brain. Who knew if his memory would improve or worsen. Besides, to her, he was just a patient. An injured bull rider with big clumsy feet that slapped the floor with each step as if they were asleep.

"Here we are." She positioned him in front of the bars.

He gripped the right bar awkwardly, adjusted his weight, let go of her arm and reached for the left. Then careened toward it.

"Whoa," she said, grabbing his arm to steady him. "Take a step and lean your hip into it for support."

His face warmed as he stepped closer, followed her instructions, and she guided his hand to the bar. The steel cooled his heated palms.

"Now you got it."

Despite her encouragement, he didn't feel like he had anything. Or ever would again.

She strode to the other end of the bars, then stepped inside, a few feet away from him. "I'm right here if you have any trouble. Now use the left side for support while you step forward with your right."

"You make it sound so easy."

"It'll get easy again. You're ahead of the game since you're all lean muscle." Her cheeks tinged pink.

She'd noticed his muscles.

"I mean muscle recovers faster than fat."

Feeling confident under her praise, he took a step forward. Then swayed.

"Not so fast." She grabbed his arm. "Slow down, Clint. Take your time. There's no marathon tomorrow. Baby steps, remember?"

And just like that, he was feeble. One bull ride had rendered him awkward and useless. For what?

"I just wish I could remember why I went back to the rodeo. I mean, this time?" The time he didn't remember. "Why did I want to buy a ranch in Fort Worth? It doesn't make any sense." He took another step. "Why would I want a ranch close to five hours away?"

"I don't know." She frowned. "I don't mean to get personal..." Her cheeks flushed. "But are you seeing anyone? Maybe from that area?"

Seeing someone? Could there be a woman he'd forgotten? "Wouldn't my family know if I was?"

"Maybe. But some people are private about that kind of thing. Until they know it's going to work or turn into something permanent."

"If there was someone in my life, wouldn't I have heard from her by now?" he asked, taking another step.

"Not if she doesn't know you're hurt. Or she's on a business trip or something."

"I don't think so." Surely he couldn't have forgotten a special woman in his life. "But I think I need to search my room. See if I can find any phone numbers, pictures." Of a woman. "Maybe the Fort Worth ranch owner's name and number. Perhaps I told him why I wanted to buy the ranch."

"Well, while you were pondering, you made it all the way through the bars. Without stumbling."

Despite himself, a spark of satisfaction spread through him. He hadn't even realized he was at the end. Lexie had backed out of the tunnel as he'd progressed, still two feet away from him. "Wow. Maybe you need to keep me distracted during therapy more often."

She smiled brightly. "I think we can stop for the day and you can go search for clues in your room." Lexie offered her arm. "Back to the chair."

He winced, dreading the chair, and touching her made him think about things he had no right to consider. Especially if there was a woman in his life. "Can I try the walker?"

"Sure. Just stay here and I'll get it." She hurried toward it.

Oh for the days when he could walk wherever he wanted without even thinking about it. Would he ever get back to what he was? At the moment, he couldn't even remember if he had a girlfriend or not.

Lexie positioned the walker in front of him. "The nonskid feet will keep you from scooting the walker and give you more support. Once you transfer your weight, you'll have to pick it up slightly with each step. Not too high, just enough to move forward. Grab on and we'll practice." She hovered close while he slowly moved forward enough to grip the right side, then the left and scoot his body inside the cage of the contraption.

He picked the walker up, then stepped forward with it, with only minor weaving.

"Very good. Is it the right height, so that it's comfortable?"

"I think so," he answered.

"I do, too. Relax your arms for a second." She ran a hand along his elbow. "Looks good."

But her touch tingled up to his shoulder, even after she took a step back.

"Keep going," she instructed.

He took another step.

"I think you've got it. Just remember, if you feel off balance, put the feet down until you're stable. And this walker has the lower grips too, for support in getting up and down from a seated position."

She opened the door into the hall and he clunked his way down it.

The walker was slow and noisy since he kept bumping the wall, but so much better than the chair.

"Well, look at you!" Carly sat at the kitchen table with Mom, who was bouncing a giggling Charlee in her lap. "All mobile and everything."

"Getting there."

"Uncle Clint." Cooper ran to him, stared at the walker.

"It's just a walker," Lexie explained. "To keep your uncle from falling until he gets his balance back."

"Kind of like Charlee's walker without all the spinning toys." Carly leaned across the table and smoothed Charlee's hair out of her face.

"Charlee has walker," the toddler chimed in.

Still surreal that Charlee existed and was talking. And walked better than he could.

"Yes, you have a walker, just like Uncle Squint." Mom smiled at her granddaughter, then turned to look at him and Lexie. "I take it therapy went well."

"He made it all the way through the parallel bars with very little wobble once he got going." Lexie made it sound like he'd won a marathon.

"That's wonderful."

"Uncle Squint?"

"Hey, Charlee." Her name tasted new on his lips. If only he could summon up memories of her.

"Pway game?"

"She wants to play Chutes and Ladders." Cooper ran to the closet where his parents had always kept board games. "We do that a lot. We use Mega Bloks instead of pawns so she doesn't put them in her mouth."

"Not in mouth." Charlee opened wide to show them.

"I'm not sure if that's a good idea." Carly cringed, obviously expecting him to be incapable. "Maybe when Uncle Clint gets a little better."

"Actually, that would be excellent therapy." Lexie assured her. "Practice on grip, cognitive skills and hand movement. Some of our therapy involves board games."

Memories hit him. Of climbing his green LEGO up ladders then sliding down chutes with Cooper. But not Charlee. And Dad had been there.

"I remember playing with you." He aimed his walker toward the game table behind the couch in the adjoining family room.

"You do?" Cooper's eyes lit up as he set the box on the table.

"You were younger, but I remember. You beat me a lot."

Cooper giggled. "Want me to let you win since your brain got jarred around and you're weird?"

"Cooper, stop calling your uncle weird," Mom scolded, setting a wiggly Charlee down.

"It's okay, I am kind of weird right now." Clint crossed his eyes and stuck his tongue out, which got a laugh from Cooper and Charlee. "I don't need your charity, even if

I'm weird. You better bring your A game if you wanna beat me, partner."

"Y'all have fun." Lexie waved. "I'll see you tomorrow."

"Pway game." Charlee grabbed Lexie's hand, then raised her arms, obviously expecting to be picked up.

Carly stood. "I'll play with you, Charlee. Lexie needs to go."

"It's okay." Lexie picked her up and planted the child on her hip. Like a natural. His heart warmed at the sight. "I'd love to. I used to play that game with my friend's little girl, and this little cutie reminds me of when she was small." She sat down at the table, settling Charlee in her lap.

Cooper set up the board as Clint continued his slow progress to the table. "I'm blue, Uncle Clint is always green and Charlee is yellow. Is red okay with you, Lexie?"

"That's what I always pick."

As if she fit right in with them.

He finally made it to the table. "Maybe one day we'll play chess."

"You already taught me, Uncle Clint." Cooper stashed the box on the kitchen counter. "But Charlee's too young."

He totally didn't remember teaching Cooper. A twinge of sadness radiated through him.

"Use the upper and lower grips to hold steady while you sit," Lexie instructed, always in therapist mode. At least she didn't get up and hover nearby.

For the first time, he managed to sit down by himself. Suddenly he saw the walker as freedom, instead of making him feel old and used up.

"Charlee always goes first, then whoever's lap she's in is next, and we go clockwise around the table," Cooper explained as he passed the spinner to Lexie. "Your turn, Charlee."

The toddler reached her plump little hand out and used her index finger to spin. Probably better than he'd do.

"You got a four!" Lexie clapped her hands. "Charlee gets to go up the ladder to fourteen." She leaned forward and counted out the blocks, then the ladder, and the fourteen with her finger as Charlee scooted her LEGO into place. "Good job, Charlee."

She sounded just like she did when she encouraged him. At least she didn't use the singsong baby talk voice with him.

"Charlee did good," his niece declared, giggling excitedly.

"You *did* do good." He needed to connect with her, even if he didn't remember her. His insides quaked. Who else had he forgotten?

"Your turn, Lexie." Cooper always kept things moving when they played.

Lexie thumped the spinner with her index finger, then moved her LEGO to the first square and promptly landed on a long ladder that took her all the way to thirty-eight.

"Wow, looks like Lexie might beat all of us." Cooper passed the spinner to Clint. "Your turn."

He tried to thump it, but couldn't.

"Just use one finger, Uncle Clint," Cooper instructed.

But Clint couldn't keep the weight of his hand off the spinner enough to make it spin. "Maybe this isn't a good idea…"

"You can do it." Lexie's gaze pinged from him to his nephew. "Cooper, can you support his hand? Just hold his wrist for him until he gets to where he can do it himself."

As if she had confidence he'd be able to soon.

Cooper grabbed Clint's wrist, suspending his hand above the spinner. "I can do it for you if you need me to, Uncle Clint."

"I think I can do it, now." He managed an awkward spin that barely made a full circle.

"Good job," Lexie encouraged. "Before you know it, you won't need any help."

He got a three. No chutes or ladders. With fumbling fingers, he managed to scoot his LEGO into place. Cooper spun an eight with no chutes or ladders.

Over their next several rounds, everyone got ladders with Charlee landing on a long ladder that shot her up to the eighty-fourth square. While Clint consistently got nothing or chutes that landed him back on lower squares. As he awkwardly spun and moved his LEGO, he had to count out each square like a toddler. But at least he remembered how to count.

Lexie continued to help Charlee with each move and clapped each time anyone made progress. In the end, Charlee won while Clint had barely gotten off the first row since he'd consistently hit the sixteenth square with the chute that slid him back to six each time.

"Yay, Charlee. You won!" Lexie announced cheerfully.

"Charlee win." The toddler giggled.

"That's right." Clint slapped his hands together like they were two dead fish, but at least he'd managed to clap. Though he'd enjoyed interacting with his niece and nephew, the game had been a series of failures for him. Typical therapy session.

"It'll get easier." Lexie patted his hand. "I need to go. My mom probably has supper on the table by now. But y'all keep playing and you'll get better and better each time."

How did she do that, read his thoughts, know just when he needed encouraging?

She stood, then set Charlee in his lap. "Thanks for being my game buddy, Charlee. Next time, let me win."

"Charlee won," Charlee repeated, clapping her hands.

He gripped his own hands around the toddler, working at keeping her steady, his nerves in a panic. What if he dropped her? He watched Lexie sling her purse over her shoulder, say her goodbyes.

No matter what a good cheerleader she was. No matter how attractive she was. He could not think of her as anything other than a therapist. Not while there was a chance he might never get better and only decline as his father had.

And especially not if he already had a girlfriend. Which was something he doubted, but he needed to find out for certain. Soon.

Chapter Seven

Clint dug through the last drawer in his room while clinging to his walker with one hand. Last night after Carly had taken the kids home, he'd searched the office at the ranch and found a business card for Fort Worth Beefalo Holdings. But it had been too late to call. He'd spent the morning searching his room for any traces of a phantom girlfriend. But the heavy, mahogany-stained dresser had yielded nothing.

A knock sounded on his door. "You sound like a big rat in there," Carly called. "Do you need help?"

"No, but come on in."

The door opened and his sister stepped inside.

"What are you doing here?"

"Mom had some errands to run, so she asked me to drop by until Lexie gets here."

He scowled. "I don't need a babysitter."

"Try telling Mom that."

"Don't you need to get to work?"

"My boss has been really good about letting me come in late when Mom needs me to. I'll make it up with short lunch breaks. So what are you doing in here?"

"Do I have a girlfriend?"

Carly's eyebrows rose. "Not that I know of. You dated

Katie back before Dad got sick, but as far as I know, there hasn't been anyone else."

Good ole Katie. Crazy about him until he had to move back home and help with Dad. Then she was done and had moved on to the next bull rider.

"Do you think there's someone special in your life?" she asked.

"No. Surely if there was, I'd have heard from her by now." It was Saturday; an entire week had passed since his accident. "Plus, I've searched my entire room and found nothing. No pictures. No contacts in my phone. No texts. Nothing."

"Then what gave you the idea that you might?"

"Lexie mentioned that if I had a girlfriend, she might be able to help me fill in some blanks. And if I was seeing someone in Fort Worth, maybe that's why I wanted to move. It hit me, that I don't know."

"Well, if you have a girlfriend, she's not a very good one. She hasn't even checked on you." She poked him in the ribs. "Maybe Lexie thinks you're cute and she can't believe you don't have someone special."

"Stop it." But the thought did something funny to his insides.

"Well, since you don't have a girlfriend, Lexie is very sweet and pretty."

"She's my therapist."

"So?"

"So there's probably some law about that, plus I can barely walk or feed myself." After almost a full week of therapy. "The last thing I need is a relationship."

"There's that. But maybe after you get well, she won't be your therapist then." Carly waggled her eyebrows.

"If I get well, I'll be busy expanding the ranch and won't have time to date."

"Stop with the if. When you get well, someday, you'll

be old and gray. And lonely. Think how much easier this setback would be if you had a wife to share it with you."

"Then I'd be a burden to someone besides you and Mom."

"You're not a burden."

The doorbell rang.

"That's probably Lexie, my *therapist*." He emphasized the word. "Can you get it?" Anything to get her off the wife subject.

Because if he had a wife, and he was following in Dad's footsteps healthwise, he'd only break her heart as he continued to go downhill.

"By the way, the vet called to confirm he's coming Monday for vaccinations," Carly called out to him on the way to the door. "And breakfast is keeping warm in the oven. I'll see you later."

Lexie stepped into the room a few moments later. "Good morning. Did you sleep well?"

"Enough." He couldn't turn his brain off for such things.

"What are you doing?" She did a slow scan of the room, taking in the pale blue walls, the drawers that still hung open.

"I'm pretty sure I don't have a girlfriend. Or she's very camera shy." Clint closed the drawer and the two next to it. "But I did find this." He held up the business card.

"Have you called them yet?"

"No, but I'm about to." He dug the cell phone from his pocket, jabbed at the numbers, but his aim was off. "Can you do it for me?"

"No. Part of therapy is learning to do things for yourself. Set the phone down on the dresser and concentrate."

With the phone stable, instead of trying to hold it and dial with the same hand, he managed to place the call. It rang three times, but it seemed like an eternity.

"Fort Worth Beefalo Holdings, can I help you?" a man inquired.

He cleared his throat. "This is Clint Rawlins."

"Hold on, Mr. Rawlins, my boss has been waiting for your call."

For how long? How many people had he left hanging?

"Mr. Rawlins, it's good of you to *finally* call me back." The man's tone radiated sarcasm. "Now do we have a deal or not?"

"I'm sorry. Who is this?"

"Who is this? Just the guy you've left hanging for almost a week. I turned down other deals, Mr. Rawlins." The guy's anger echoed through the line.

"Let me." Lexie reached for the phone.

Feeling completely inept, Clint handed it over.

"Hi, my name is Lexie Parker. I'm an occupational therapist and Mr. Rawlins is my patient. Is it okay if I put you on speakerphone? Only Mr. Rawlins and I are here." She shot him a reassuring smile. "Thank you." Lexie pressed the button. "Who am I speaking with?"

"This here's Franklin Thomas. Now what's going on?"

The name didn't mean a thing to Clint.

"Mr. Rawlins was in a bull riding accident at the rodeo. He's suffering some short-term memory loss. He only knows he was thinking about buying your ranch because his family told him and he just found your business card last night."

Short-term memory loss that claimed a two-year chunk of his life.

"Are you shooting straight with me? Or is this a front for him backing out of the deal?"

"I can assure you, I'm telling you the truth, Mr. Thomas." Her tone was firm, but kind. "And in light of his current circumstances, I recommend that your deal with Mr. Rawlins be tabled."

A pregnant pause.

"Sure thing. I wouldn't want to buy a ranch if I couldn't remember why I wanted it."

"Thank you." She cleared her throat. "Mr. Rawlins would like to ask you a few questions if you have time."

"Of course."

She took the call off speaker and handed him the phone back.

"I apologize for leaving you hanging with our deal, Mr. Thomas."

"Perfectly understandable under the circumstances." Though Mr. Thomas was probably still frustrated, it didn't come across in his tone. "I'm sorry you're having to deal with this and for being short with you."

"Did I ever say why I wanted to buy your ranch, sir?"

"No. Just that you wanted to expand your beefalo business," the man answered. "I have to agree with your therapist—it would be foolhardy to go through with the deal if you can't even remember what your purpose was."

Clint sighed. "I'm sorry I let you down."

"No worries. But I can't hold the ranch for you. I do have other buyers interested."

"I understand," he replied. "You do what you need to do. And if I get my brain sorted out soon, I'll let you know."

"I hope you make a full recovery."

"Thank you. Me, too." Clint's eyes watered up as he ended the call.

"If you get better?" Lexie's right eyebrow lifted. "Attitude is half the battle. You cannot think *if*, Clint. You have to think *when*."

"That's exactly what Carly said this morning." He blinked away the moisture. "I'll try."

"Where's your mom?"

"Carly said she's running errands. She left really early, though."

Her lips quirked up into a smile. "Maybe she's stir-crazy."

"Or maybe she's with Ted."

"I have an idea," Lexie said.

He knew she was trying to distract him from the Ted situation, but he was all ears.

"What do you have in mind?"

"If you work really hard today, maybe we can take some of your therapy sessions outside next week and make sure *you* don't go stir-crazy."

"Sure, I'm up for it. But why not today?"

"I think you need a little more work on the balance ball and the bars first. But come Monday, we'll go for a walk. With your walker. Traversing uneven ground is excellent therapy and you could use some fresh air and sunlight."

It sounded like a great idea and he needed the distraction. Something to look forward to as whatever life he'd lived before crumbled around him.

Lexie stepped onto the porch of the Rawlins ranch and rang the bell. Church had been nice, seeing people she hadn't seen in a while, and she'd looked forward to avoiding Clint's charm for the rest of the day. But she couldn't let his mom down. Audrey needed a family outing and to know that Clint would be fine, so she could enjoy it.

Long minutes passed before a clunking noise sounded on the other side. Clint's walker.

The door opened. He wore his typical track pants and T-shirt like he did on their therapy days.

"You ready?"

"For what?" He frowned. "I thought this was your—our—day off."

"No therapy today. You did great yesterday, so your reward is a picnic lunch." She stepped inside and hung her purse on the hall tree. "Cooper wanted everybody to go to the Old Spanish Trail for lunch. Apparently that's something y'all usually do on Sunday after church. But your mom didn't want you to be alone any longer." She hurried to the kitchen as his walker thunked along lagging behind her.

"I can take care of myself." His tone turned defensive.

"I know that. And you know that. But she doesn't know that. You're her baby boy and you're hurt. I promised to come here so they could go and she wouldn't worry." Lexie winced. She probably should have skipped the part about the family lunch. Even though he knew about Ted now, Clint might still be struggling with the new man in Audrey's life. But if he felt left out of the family gathering, he wasn't showing it.

"Is that what you wore to church?"

"I wear jeans to Wednesday night Bible study since it's casual, but not for Sunday service. I stopped by the house and changed." She dug around in the refrigerator. "I thought we could warm up that soup your mom made for lunch yesterday and enjoy the pretty day."

"I'm all about leftover tortilla soup and being outside."

"Me, too. Do you know where your mom keeps plastic bowls with lids?" She found the Pyrex dish full of soup along with the pan of cornbread. Then she cut two nice-sized pieces, put them on a plate and zapped them in the microwave.

"Used to be in here." He opened a cabinet. "Yep. How many you need?"

"Three." She ladled the soup into a glass bowl, took the cornbread out of the microwave and put the soup in. "What about a thermos?"

"Bottom cabinet on the other side of the dishwasher."

"Think you can put the cornbread in a bowl for us?" She dug the thermos out, poured tea into it from the pitcher kept in the Rawlinses' fridge.

"I'll try not to dump it all in the floor." He clunked his way to the table and set three bowls and lids down.

It hadn't taken him as long to collect them as she'd expected.

"Give it a whirl." She dug a set of tongs out of a drawer, set them and the bowl of warmed bread on the table. "Don't stress over it. If it's too hard or frustrates you, I can take over. But sit down to do it."

"Good idea." He kerplunked into a chair.

She watched out of the corner of her eye as he worked the tongs, using both hands, a frown creasing his forehead. Not so firm a grip that he crumbled the cornbread, she noted. He successfully transferred it into the bowl. Very impressive.

The bell dinged on the microwave and she retrieved the warmed soup, then sat across the table from him to place each helping in the plastic containers.

Just a few crumbs dotted the table as Clint snapped the lids on his bowls. He stood, thudded over to the sink and grabbed a dishcloth, then came back and slowly wiped the mild mess into his other hand. Without dropping any, he went over to the trash can and threw it away.

"Do you realize what you just did?"

"Cleaned up my own mess. Did Mom tell you where the picnic basket is?"

"No. I was planning on using a grocery bag."

"Not around here. She's got the white-and-red-checked blanket and the whole shebang with plates, cups and utensils in the basket. We used to go camping a lot when Carly and I were kids."

"I've never been camping," she admitted.

"A travesty."

"Not really. I don't like bugs. I really prefer heated or air-conditioned premises, and plumbing is a must."

He chuckled. “Typical female. We had a camper with air, heat and plumbing.”

“I might could go for that.”

“She used to keep the basket in the foyer closet. I’ll go take a look.” He plodded toward the front of the house.

She could have done it much faster. But he needed to do things on his own when he could. Especially with the progress he was making.

By the time he came back carrying a basket with the checked blanket folded on top, she had their lunch lined up on the table.

“Looks like we’re all set,” she murmured, stowing the items in the basket. “Ready?”

“We better not go far. As slowly as I move, the food will be cold.”

“You’re really doing great.” She made a point to meet his gaze, even though the intensity of his green eyes did a number on her pulse. “Can you imagine doing that professional cornbread transfer when you first got home?”

“No.”

“Yesterday at lunch, you got very little soup on your shirt and you cleaned up your very minor mess just now.”

“I did, didn’t I.” He smiled and it reached his eyes for the first time since she’d met him.

Oh, those eyes.

She turned away. “Let’s go. Time’s a-wasting.”

They made their way slowly outside. “I’m thinking under that live oak is the perfect picnic spot.” And it was only a few yards from the back of the house.

“Maybe we could go on that walk after we eat?”

“Baby steps,” she reminded him. “This is your prologue to the walk tomorrow.”

“Is this a test? And if I fail, I don’t get to walk?”

“No. It’s a practice run.”

He made it to the steps. The walker was twice as deep

as each porch step, leaving the apparatus with two feet suspended in the air.

"Hold up, I've got it." Lexie set down the basket and held his walker steady, countering with her weight.

Then reality hit. "Why does everything have to be so hard?" Clint grumbled.

"It won't be hard for long. Right?"

"Right." But his tone came out flat.

"I've got you, I promise."

"How can that be? I outweigh you."

"Surely you don't think this is my first rodeo. I've had patients who outweighed you." Poor guy. Afraid to step off the porch. A task he used to do without thinking. "Trust me."

Clint shuffled one foot down, then the other.

"Perfect. Now set the walker on the next one."

He tipped forward, but she steadied the walker, and him.

Slowly, painfully he progressed until he stood on the sidewalk. His face was flushed. From effort or embarrassment? Probably a little bit of both.

As they inched their way down the walk, his coloring returned to normal.

"You shouldn't be embarrassed." She slowed her stride to match his halting movements. "You're not clumsy or awkward. Your brain just doesn't remember how to make your hands and feet move right. Just for now. But we're teaching, retraining your brain. The only way you'd have any right to be embarrassed would be if you went to bed and didn't try."

"You've had patients like that?"

"Too many," she admitted.

"What happened to them?" A tendon in his jaw tensed.

"They're still in bed."

They made it to the shade and Lexie spread the blanket out, placed the picnic basket in the middle.

"Maybe I should have brought chairs." She hadn't really thought about him trying to get down to the ground.

"I've got this."

"The best way—"

But he'd already turned his walker around, bent, gripped the lower bars, then lowered to his knees and onto his hip.

"Wow! You did that exactly like I was about to instruct you."

He shrugged but she could tell that her praise pleased him. "I've had some practice when you weren't here. In fact, I googled how to do a few things."

"You're getting very self-sufficient." She opened the basket, handed him a warm bowl, divvied out the utensils and cornbread, then poured their teas.

"Thanks to you."

"And Google."

"If only my memory would progress." He blessed the food with a thankful prayer and a petition to restore his mind and body.

"So what did you plan to do with your time off between jobs?" Clint hadn't missed his mouth or dropped anything yet.

"I have no idea. Everybody in my life thought I needed time off, so I was doing it to appease them." She sighed. "I tend to put everything into my job and have very little social life. It works for me, but my parents and friends are certain I'll burn myself out. I'd honestly have been bored to tears with a month and no job."

"So I saved you from boredom."

"Yes and I appreciate it. Do you remember what you used to like to do in your free time?"

He frowned, obviously trying to remember, overthinking her simple question.

"From what I remember, I usually stayed so busy with the ranch that I didn't have any spare daylight. But I liked to go camping. I even considered buying a camper several years ago. Back before Dad got sick, before the ranch became my sole responsibility."

"The ranch is doing well now. And you've had a week off already. When we get you back to a hundred percent, you should buy that camper. In fact, I heard you've got a rodeo purse to spend."

"I could do that." His eyes lit up. "Maybe I will if—*when*—I recover. And I could introduce you to camping. I mean, not together. Well sort of. You could sleep in the camper and I'd make a tent if you wanted to go sometime."

"That actually sounds fun." It sounded dreamy. Spending time with him once he was whole again. But when he fully recovered, he'd probably travel the rodeo circuit with his camper. "But by then, I'll be busy with my new job."

"Do you think we'll see each other once my therapy is over?" he asked.

"If we both stick around here. Medina is a very small town." But that was all it could be. Seeing one another in passing. Even when he fully recovered physically and he wasn't her patient any longer, she couldn't trust a relationship built on a patient having a crush on his therapist. And especially not if the emotion and decision-making aspects of his brain were permanently damaged.

Tread carefully and keep her heart out of it.

"This is where Carly used to try to make me have tea parties with her when we were kids." He tilted his head back and looked up into the branches of the gigantic tree.

"Sounds like some rough childhood you had there."

"Ha ha," he shot back. "But in all seriousness, I know I was very blessed. I look back now and realize she just wanted to spend time with her little brother." Suddenly he grimaced. "All my friends had brothers, so back then I thought I was cursed with only a sister. I could have been nicer, found something we could play together."

"Little boys don't think like adults, though."

He turned toward her. "How about you? Any brothers or sisters?"

"Nope. Just me."

"Was that lonely for you?"

"Not at all," she answered. "I had my friend, Larae. Since my parents worked at her ranch, I went there every day after school. So we were constantly together, practically like sisters."

"And Larae lives here?"

"She just moved back last year. I got to sit with her at church this morning, along with another friend of ours. It was great for all of us to be there together again."

He finished his last spoonful of soup and his cornbread was long gone.

"We better get back to the house," she said.

"Can't we stay out here?"

"I think Carly is bringing the kids to see you. So I'll head home, spend some time with my folks and see you tomorrow." She put her bowl back in the basket.

"Let me." He picked up each of his items and placed them back carefully into the basket. With a tight grip on the lower bar of his walker, he leaned on his hip and started to get on his knees. But he lost his balance and fell back on his hip.

"Here." She stood, offering him her hand.

But he shooed her away. "I can do it," he snapped. "Just go back to the house."

"Are you sure?"

"Positive."

She nodded. "I'll get the basket and the blanket."

"Leave the blanket. If it's the last thing I do, I'm folding it by myself and bringing it back to the house."

"Okay." She grabbed the basket and turned toward the

house. Leaving him there went against everything she wanted to do. But he was determined.

She stepped inside the back door and watched from the kitchen window. Another try to get up landed him on his hip again. Two more tries before he managed to get on his knees. He looped the corner of the blanket on the side rail of his walker, then stood. Then with one hand, he picked the blanket up.

There was no way he could fold the blanket and hold on to his walker, too. She winced as he struggled. With everything in her, she wanted to help instead of stand back and watch, but she knew he needed to figure things out on his own in order to regain his independence.

"Lexie?" Audrey's voice came from behind her.

She jumped and spun.

"What are you doing?"

"We had a picnic." Lexie filled her in on how well Clint had done, until the trouble he'd encountered with standing up.

"It breaks my heart, too." Audrey fished a tissue out of her purse and handed it to Lexie.

Why was she crying? She dabbed her eyes. "It just reminds me of Levi." She covered.

"Me, too. But Clint will be fine. Thanks to you. You're the most caring therapist I've ever known."

"Thank you." She sighed. "I better go since I promised to spend some time with my parents today."

"I appreciate you keeping him company on your day off. See you tomorrow. I'll make sure he makes it inside okay."

Lexie had been told she cared too much. That she got too attached. But this was different. This time, she was smitten with a brain-damaged patient who was incapable of making sound decisions. So even if she was reading him correctly and he was interested in her, there could never be anything between them.

Chapter Eight

Though Clint had made it down the steps with more confidence today, Lexie had to slow her pace, forcing herself to wait on him.

"Where are we going?"

"To the barn. I want to see these beefalo you raise." The structure loomed in the distance.

"You can go ahead. You don't have to wait for me. It'll take me half a day to get there."

She flashed him a grin. "Not quite that long and I don't mind."

His next several slow-motion steps echoed with the thwack of his walker accompanied by bird chatter in the breeze.

"Was my dad embarrassed when he couldn't do things?"

"Sometimes. At first."

"He'd be upset if he was still here and he knew I went back to the rodeo even after what happened to him."

"Maybe," she acknowledged. "But I'm sure he'd be worried about you more than anything."

He blew out a big breath. "I don't know what I was thinking."

Sure, he was remorseful now, after a bull had cost him memories for two years of his life and taken away the ability to do simple tasks he'd done before without thinking. But what about once he recovered his physical and mental abilities? Was he a rodeo junkie?

"So is my mom sneaking off to see Ted?"

"I honestly don't know." She needed to tread carefully. *Lord, give me the words.* "I do know that he comforts her. And when he offered to stay away until you're reconciled to things as they are, the doctor said he didn't need to avoid your mom, that she'd need him."

"Is he as good a guy as my dad?"

"Well, I've only been around him a few times. But he seems great. And I doubt your mom would be engaged to anyone who wasn't."

They made it to the steel rail fence. Several huge female beefalo with curly foreheads surrounded a massive bull.

A ranch hand near the barn waved. They returned the gesture.

"I don't know that guy." Clint set his walker aside and hooked his elbows over the fence. "From what I've seen, none of the hands I remember are still around."

"You can get to know them. Until you remember."

Metal clanks and bawling echoed from the barn. A reminder that the vet was there and the beefalo obviously weren't happy with their plight.

"So why beefalo?"

"Some years Medina is really dry. Beefalo aren't picky grazers and don't require grain, so they're easier and cheaper to raise. They're hardier in extreme heat or cold and the meat is leaner with low fat and cholesterol. They breed longer and have easier births and they're docile, like cows."

"Docile?" she scoffed. "I've been chased by cows a few times in my life. I don't think they're docile at all. In fact, they're evil."

"Evil?" He chuckled. "Cows?"

"It all happened at my best friend Larae's ranch, where my parents work. Daddy is the foreman and Mama is the cook. When I was nine, Larae and I were at the river with my poodle. The cow was on the other side. She kept staring at us, creeping closer, until I grabbed Gigi up and we ran back to the ranch house." She rolled her eyes. "My parents said she was curious about my dog, but that cow chased us all the way back to the house."

Clint clamped his mouth shut, in a poor attempt to contain his amusement.

"Then just a few years ago, I was home for a visit and happened to be at the ranch again. Daddy had a cow out, so I thought I'd be brave and help him. All I did was tell her she didn't need to get in the road. But she came charging toward me.

"I ran, but I had flip-flops on and stepped in an armadillo hole. I managed to get behind an old fence Daddy had replaced and was tearing down in sections, so it was open at both ends. She reared up and flailed her hooves at me, then started around after me. Thankfully, Daddy got her attention by banging on the feed bucket and got her back in the fence."

His struggle ended and he roared with laughter.

"Daddy said she wanted to play, but I've never owned a pair of flip-flops again. I only wear tennis shoes or comfortable boots when I go anywhere cows are." At least her most embarrassing moments had gotten Clint to temporarily forget his problems. "And I keep a fence between them and me."

"I'm sorry your parents took the cow's side both times." He grinned.

"I really hadn't thought about it that way."

A man exited the barn, wearing coveralls and muck boots.

"Hey, Jerry." Lexie waved at Jerry Booth, Medina's vet for as long as she could remember.

"Why, Lexie Parker, aren't you a sight for sore eyes. I was wondering what all the laughter was about out here."

"I hope we didn't cause a distraction," Clint said, adjusting his weight against the fence.

"Not at all." Jerry's gaze pinged back and forth between the two of them. "I'm glad to see Lexie finally has a social life. Clint here is a good man."

"We're not…" Lexie's face heated. "We're just friends."

"Oh. Pardon my manners for assuming."

"How's the herd?" Clint asked.

"Healthy." Jerry strolled over and held a bill out toward Clint.

Clint let go of the fence with one arm, reached for it and lost his balance.

But Lexie was there to steady him. His face turned scarlet.

"You all right, Clint?" The vet furrowed his brow in concern.

"Just a little bull wreck. But I'm mending."

"Oh." Jerry's gaze cut to Lexie. "Well, you got the best therapist friend in Medina. Lexie will have you healed up in no time."

"Thanks, Jerry." Lexie took the bill and stuffed it in her pocket without looking at it. Trying to leave Clint some semblance of privacy.

With a wave, Jerry strode around the back of the barn. An engine started up and minutes later, the white mobile veterinarian vehicle pulled into sight. Jerry waved again as he continued down the drive and exited the property.

"Ready to go back inside?" she asked.

"Absolutely not. Let's walk some more."

"All right. A little farther, but we don't want to tire you out."

"I'm good. Better out here."

"Okay." She positioned his walker for him, steadied him while he transferred his weight from the fence.

Maybe getting him outside *had* been just what the doctor ordered.

Light tugged at Clint's heavy eyelids. He squinted them open. Daylight streamed through a crack between the curtains. Morning. In his bedroom at the ranch. He peered at the pale blue walls, trying to gather his thoughts. Why was Dad's walker by his bed?

Oh, yeah. It wasn't Dad's.

He closed his eyes.

Two and a half years had passed since Dad had been gone. Cooper was seven. Charlee was almost two. Mom was engaged and sneaking around to see her boyfriend. Like a teenager. Because of him. He needed to find the strength to fix that.

Yesterday, he'd gotten to go outside to check on his herd. To take a walk with Lexie. Why had the vet thought they were a couple? He could count the reasons they shouldn't be. She was his therapist. He was currently disabled and couldn't even stand up without a walker. His condition could be permanent and on a downhill spiral.

Clothes were folded neatly on his side table, courtesy of Mom. Sitting on the side of his bed, he managed to tug on the pair of lightweight stretchy pants and a matching T-shirt.

The doorbell rang. She was here.

He made slow progress with his walker down the hall, into the kitchen.

"Good morning." She smiled.

That did something funny to his heart.

He returned her greeting.

The bright colors of her turquoise-and-purple scrubs

complimented her exotic coloring. The pattern was like the swirls sometimes carved in saddle leather or on a handkerchief. Like Mom's couch. What had she called it? Paisley, yeah that was it. Why did he care?

"I have an appointment." Mom set his plate on the table. Eggs, bacon and biscuits.

"So early?" He managed to make it to the table, support himself on the surface and fall heavily into his chair. "Are you sneaking out to see Ted again?"

Mom's face turned red.

"It's okay, Mom. You're not a child and you shouldn't have to sneak around to see someone you obviously love. I want to meet him."

His mom's eyes lit up, but then a frown pinched between her brows, and she turned to Lexie. "Do you think that's a good idea?"

"If Clint is up for it, I think it's an excellent idea."

"I'll see when he can come over for supper then," Mom said with a smile.

He'd clearly made her day. And it was about time for him to do something besides worry her.

"Is it okay if I still meet him for breakfast at the Old Spanish Trail, since we already had it planned?" Mom set her purse down. "Or would you rather I stay here? I can if you want me to."

"You don't have to ask my permission and no more planning things around me."

"You're the best son." She kissed his temple.

But he hadn't been. He'd gone back to bull riding. Twice. Even though it worried her. Despite what the sport had done to Dad. Why? He had to find out what had pushed him to go back this time.

"What do you want for supper when Ted comes?" she asked.

He swallowed hard. "Fix something he likes."

Mom beamed, waved her fingers and went out the door to the garage.

"That was very considerate of you," Lexie murmured, taking a seat across from him.

"I figure I've put her through enough." Now he just needed to stomach the meeting with Ted. "Let me pray over the food."

Lexie bowed her head.

"Thank You, Lord, for my mom. For my family. For a good therapist. Help me to get through supper with Ted. Let him be the man my mom needs. Allow me to fully recover so I can be a help to my family instead of a hindrance. Bless this food and thank You for all the blessings You give us. In Jesus's name, amen."

He raised his head to see Lexie smiling at him. "What?"

"Out of all my patients, you're my second praying one. Your dad was the first."

A knot formed in his throat. "I'm embarrassed I hadn't thought to do it before now."

"God understands. The brain thing." She pointed to his head. "Levi was a wonderful man." She covered his hand with hers.

Their gazes caught, held. She jerked her hand away.

At her fleeting touch, all the reasons they'd make a great couple echoed through his mind. She was a Christian. She was caring, encouraging and trustworthy. On top of that, she was beautiful. Since Dad died, he'd been so focused on the ranch he hadn't thought about his future. Not that he remembered, anyway. Marriage? Kids? Lexie made him want to think on it.

But a couple of big ifs stood in their way. If he could get well. Recover everything he'd lost. If he didn't have permanent brain damage like his dad. Then what? Could Lexie be interested in him? Or did she see him only as a patient?

"Want me to stick around for dinner when Ted comes? I

mean—it's up to you. If you think me being around might ease things. Keep you from feeling like a third wheel and all that."

Third wheel. Something about the phrase struck a chord of memory.

"Or I can just go, leave it to family. Or maybe see if Carly can come..."

"I'd like for you to join us." Hoping to distract himself, he jabbed a bite of eggs into his mouth.

She glanced up at him. "Don't look now, but you just found your mouth. On the first try."

His gaze dropped to her mouth. Then to his plate as he jabbed another bite. Into his cheek.

"Concentrate."

"Right. I don't want to stick whatever Mom cooks up in my ear in front of Ted."

"Your aim's not that bad." She grinned.

If he kept thinking about her lips, it might be. "Can we go outside again today?"

"Yes. If you promise to sit part of the time. We can play a card game to help with your hand movement and your memory."

"I'm in." Maybe the fresh air would keep her sweet, coconut scent at bay.

Lexie rang the bell the next evening. After a full day with Clint, she'd rushed home to change for dinner. Had she overdressed? She ran her hands down her thighs, smoothing her gauzy red-and-white polka dot blouse, which she'd paired with jeans and red, low-heeled sandals. Great, she'd invited herself and overdressed.

The door swung open, revealing a smiling Audrey. "Lexie. I'm so glad you could come. I'm so nervous and Clint is, too. You have a very soothing presence."

"Thank you." That was all she'd wanted to do—to help.

"And you look lovely."

"You do, too."

Audrey wore a cute turquoise top that brought out her pale blue eyes. With her brunette, shoulder-length hair and kind features, she was a beautiful woman. Inside and out.

"I was worried I might be overdressed. But I'm planning to attend Wednesday night Bible study after the meal."

"Which is exactly why I planned an early supper. Ted and I are planning to go, as well." Audrey ushered her inside. "I'm on pins and needles. I guess it's not every evening my son gets to meet my fiancé." Chuckling, she shook her head. *"Again."*

"Can I help you with the meal?"

"The lasagna is done and staying warm in the oven. But I haven't put the salad together yet."

Lexie followed her to the kitchen. The ranch-style house was large and airy, but somehow still cozy with lots of family photos and personal touches.

While Audrey cut up the lettuce, Lexie sliced and diced tomatoes.

"Do you think Clint's memory is getting any better?" Audrey raked lettuce off the cutting board into a large bowl.

"I'm not sure. Sometimes, I think I see flashes in his expression, like maybe he's remembering something."

"I hope so."

"He's definitely doing better physically, though. He never would have agreed to eat in front of anyone a week ago. And I think his balance has improved, too, especially since we've spent the last few days outside."

"He's always been happiest outdoors." Audrey checked her watch. "He's in the shower. I'm so glad we had the guest bathroom set up for handicapped access when Levi got sick. The more Clint can do on his own, the happier he is."

"Typical male. They tend to get more frustrated with physical limitations than women. In my experience with patients anyway."

"Especially if their last name is Rawlins." Audrey smiled. "Levi could be a bear when things didn't go like he wanted."

"But he was a teddy bear most of the time."

Audrey squeezed her arm. "I hope Clint likes Ted. Do you think we should put the wedding off? I don't want to do anything that will set my boy back in his progress."

"My gut says no. But maybe you should wait and see how tonight goes."

"Good idea."

A door opened down the hallway. "Is Lexie back yet, Mom?" Clint called.

"Yes, dear. She's right here."

"I'll see if he needs help." Lexie darted down the hall.

With his dark hair still damp, slightly tousled, Clint stood in the doorway of the guest bathroom, which apparently connected to the therapy room and his bedroom. Gone were his typical track pants and T-shirt. Instead, he wore jeans, boots and a Western shirt. And he was way, way too handsome.

He gave her a sheepish look. "I usually shave every morning, but since I may slit my throat if I try that, I decided to grow a beard. But it's getting out of hand. I look scruffy."

He looked anything but scruffy.

"I know it's not in your job description, but can you help?"

"You're in luck. My parents were both bunged up in a fender bender once and I had to shave my dad." She'd been so scared when her grandmother had told her they were in a wreck. "It came right after my friend Stacia lost her mom to a heart attack and Larae's mom died after a car wreck. I'm so blessed to still have both of my parents."

Moisture glimmered in his eyes. "I'm blessed to still have my mom."

"Do you want it all off?" She hoped not. The beard added to that tall, dark and handsome thing he had going on. But then again, maybe she needed to talk him into a clean shave so he wouldn't look so good. Who was she kidding? His handsome wasn't going anywhere.

"Not necessarily. I figure a beard is easier to maintain for now."

"Do you have clippers with a guard?"

"In that drawer, but there's some childproof thingy on it and I can't open it."

She sidestepped him, opened the drawer and dug through it. "Aha, this should do it." She pulled out his set of clippers with several guards and turned so he could see them.

"Use the closest guard. That way it'll need done less often."

"All right." She slid the guard onto the clippers. "Come stand over the sink."

"Sorry. I'd feel like such a baby if I asked Mom," he admitted, shuffling toward her as she hopped up to sit on the counter by the sink.

"It's okay." Except that she'd have to get way too close to his ruggedly handsome face to complete the task. She needed distraction to get through this. "I decided to become an occupational therapist because of my parents' accident. Because my dad was so embarrassed for me to shave him, it made me want to fix him so he could do it himself."

"How old were you?" He made it to the sink, set his walker aside and leaned on the countertop with both hands.

"Fourteen, so I might be rusty." She waggled her eyebrows at him.

"Should I be scared?"

"Nah, I can't cut you with the guard on." She put a towel over the sink and her lap, then wrapped a second towel around his broad shoulders. The clippers buzzed as she ran them over his jawline. "Just hold really still."

"You mean now's not the time to lose my balance?"

"Not unless you want a really short haircut, too. And no talking, either." She finished one side, gripped his chin and turned him to face her. His beard was soft against her fingers as she ran the clippers over his chin and mustache. What would it feel like against her lips? Her pulse spiked. Forcing herself not to make eye contact, she turned his other cheek toward her and made two swipes.

"Perfect." He turned to the mirror. "Thank you."

Lexie started breathing again. "Any time." But she hoped it grew back super slow. She used a dry washcloth to swipe over his face and knock off any loose whiskers, then carefully removed the towel from around his shoulders. "You go on to the kitchen. I'll clean up here."

"I'd argue, but I'd just spill it in the floor and make a bigger mess." He gripped his walker and gave her a rueful smile. "I couldn't sneak up on anybody if I wanted to."

"You will be able to clean up after yourself and walk normally. I'm not finished with you yet."

As he exited the bathroom, it didn't sound like he hit the walls as much as he had initially. Progress.

But Lexie needed it to happen faster. She'd only worked with him for a week and a half and she was already imagining kissing him.

Sighing, she slipped off the counter, carefully shook the towel contents into the trash, then looked in the mirror.

"No," she said aloud, jabbing a finger at her reflection. "You *cannot* fall for him. He's a patient, a rodeo junkie suffering from a brain injury that keeps him from making sound decisions. Off-limits. *So* not what you need."

Maybe Carly could help with any future grooming needs he might have. Or Ted. She had to take a step back, be objective, be a therapist. And draw the line right where it needed to be drawn.

Chapter Nine

Clint felt like a loser, sitting at the kitchen table while Lexie cleaned his whiskers off the bathroom sink. After having to trim his beard for him. His mood did not improve as he watched Mom fill drink glasses and set dishes on the table. He'd always helped her in the kitchen. But at the moment, he was pretty useless.

"Ted should be here any minute," his mother said for the fifteenth time. Obviously nervous.

"Calm down, Mom. I won't bite him."

Her laugh came out too high-pitched. "I just want you to like him."

"You said I liked him. I mean before."

"I think you did," she answered. "Or you did a good job of pretending."

"You know I don't fake it well."

"True." Mom stopped, set her hand on his shoulder. "You must have really liked him, then."

The bell rang.

"Guess he forgot his key."

Mom shot him *the look*. "He doesn't use his key except when I'm not here. And he only came to check on the house that day. To make sure the water pipes hadn't burst or anything." She scurried toward the door, then stopped and turned back to him. "If I wanted to let Ted use his key, I would. But I'd never let him move in or do anything inappropriate. I'm a Christian."

"I know. The whole thing's just weird for me."

"I'm sorry," she murmured.

"Don't be. Go let him in."

The bell rang again and she disappeared into the foyer.

Moments later, he heard whispers of conversation he couldn't make out. Then silence. Was this Ted guy kissing his mom? Clint frowned. Probably, since they were engaged.

There was movement in the hallway and then Lexie entered the kitchen. Looking gorgeous as ever. The soft, flowing, polka-dotted top accentuated her dark coloring and femininity. And she'd somehow managed to trim his beard without getting all whiskery.

"Ted's here. Mom went to let him in. I think they're kissing."

"Stop frowning. For your mom's sake."

It took effort to smooth his expression into something he hoped was calm.

Footsteps sounded in the foyer. Mom entered first.

Clint's gaze fell to Ted's hand—holding his mom's, then back to his face.

"Clint, this is Ted." Mom's smile was too cheery.

"Nice to meet you, Clint."

"Except that we've met before."

"I guess I'm not very memorable."

That squeezed a grin out of Clint.

Mom and Lexie both chuckled.

Ice slightly broken.

"Sit down, Ted." Mom gestured him to the seat that was usually hers. "Everything's ready."

"Are Carly and the kids coming?"

"No. Joel's supposed to call tonight and Carly didn't

want to take the chance of missing him, so it's just us." Mom set the salad on the table and sat down in Dad's spot with Ted on her left and Clint on her right and Lexie beside him.

"Will you bless the food, Ted?"

Clint bowed his head. Ted wasn't in Dad's seat, but Dad or Clint had always been the one to pray over their meal. He blew out a silent breath, tried to steel his nerves. *Do this for Mom.*

"Amen." Ted ended the prayer, which Clint hadn't heard any of. But at least he was a praying man.

"If everyone will pass their plates to the right, Lexie will serve the salad and I'll divvy out the lasagna." Mom sounded positively giddy.

And she had a right to. No more sneaking around. She'd probably felt like a child for the last week.

Because of him.

"Ted, you can serve the garlic bread."

Because Clint would dump it in the floor.

"So, Ted, you own Townsend Gas & Oil?" Great, that sounded like *So, Ted, you're loaded.*

"My grandfather struck oil back in the 1940s and started the company. He passed it on to my dad, who passed it on to me and my sister when he retired. Though my dad is still on the board of directors."

Born with a silver spoon in his mouth. Never had to worry a day in his life. At least Mom would be taken care of. She'd never have to fret about losing the ranch again.

"Oh, my, Audrey. This lasagna is *delicious*. And your salad rocks, Lexie." Ted shot her a wink.

"That was all Audrey, too." Lexie chuckled. "All I did was slice tomatoes."

"I feel like I'm at an Italian restaurant, only better," Ted said, smiling at Mom.

The way he looked at her. Like Dad used to. And he seemed like a nice guy.

"Without that blaring big-band music." Mom clasped a hand to her heart. "Why do they play that in Italian restaurants?"

"So do you put a lot of work hours in?" Clint tried to steer the conversation back to learning more about Ted.

"Not as much as I used to. I backed off a decade ago, so my wife and I could enjoy life. I'm glad I did, since she's gone now." A sadness washed over the older man's face, making his mouth droop at the corners.

"After Maryann's death, I went back for a time, to keep my mind busy. But then I met this little lady." Ted's eyes turned bright again with a fond look aimed at Mom. "My sister and her husband, along with my niece and nephew, handle the bulk of daily operations now."

Okay, he loved Mom. And she obviously adored him. Dad would want her to be happy. And not alone. But what about this sister, niece and nephew? Would they give Mom any trouble? Treat her like an interloper? Or worse, think she was a gold digger?

"I'd love to meet your family sometime."

"Uh, sure. That can be arranged." Ted grinned.

Clint glanced at Mom. Her smile didn't reach her eyes anymore.

"Let me guess. I've already met them."

"Apparently, they aren't very memorable, either." Ted shrugged.

Clint chuckled. And Mom's eyes lit up.

"What do they think of you and Mom? Together, I mean."

"Well, my sister, Susan, was with me when I saw your mom at church. In fact, my nephew, Josh, caught me making eyes at her. And Kathryn, my niece, made me go over and introduce myself. They're all happy that I'm happy."

"I'm glad everybody's happy." He'd just have to be, too.

"You could reacquaint yourself with Josh and Kathryn at church tonight."

Mom shook her head. "I'm afraid that might be a bit overwhelming since we have so many new members and Clint was very active in his singles class."

Wow. He couldn't even go to church.

"Maybe another dinner, then. Perhaps next time at my place. Or Kathryn's. She loves to cook."

"Maybe I'll wake up tomorrow and remember everything."

"That would be awesome," Mom said. "But there's no rush on that precious brain of yours. It'll come around."

He hoped so. It had to.

"I can stay with Clint, so you can go to Bible study tonight, Audrey," Lexie offered.

"I don't need a babysitter. You go to church with your family. Is that fiery Amarillo preacher I like still on the radio? I couldn't find him last Sunday."

Mom's eyes promptly got teary.

"What? He didn't die, did he?"

"No. Preston Hill is still very much alive and on a different station than he used to be. But you only started listening to him a year or so ago."

"So?"

"You just had a memory." Lexie smiled.

"Really?"

Ted clapped his hands in applause.

"I knew Lexie could help you." Mom dabbed tears.

"I can't take credit for that one." Lexie held her hand up for a high five.

He smacked it, straight on. And he hadn't missed his mouth once during the meal.

Maybe his brain wasn't as badly boggled as he'd thought.

* * *

Exhausted after a mostly sleepless night, Clint lay in bed staring at the ceiling. Lexie having to trim his beard for him last night and the stressful dinner had gotten the best of him.

What had he been thinking? He couldn't even groom himself or clean up the mess afterward. Why would Lexie want anything to do with him?

Stop thinking about her. Focus on recovery.

Even though the dinner had been rough on him, he'd had a memory and Ted seemed really great.

Frustration roiled through him. He could not bear the thought of staying like this. Dependent on others to tend to his most basic needs. Even if he never got the bulk of his memory back, even if his mind continued to deteriorate as Dad's had, he needed to be physically able.

With effort, he managed to sit up in his bed and hang his feet over the side. Abandoned, his Bible lay on his bedside table. Unread since he'd gotten home. Maybe even before that. Had he read it for the last two years? He couldn't remember.

He picked it up, flipped it open, started at the top of the page. *These things I have spoken unto you, that in me ye might have peace. In the world ye shall have tribulation: but be of good cheer; I have overcome the world.* John 16:33 spoke directly to him.

"Lord, I need You to help me overcome my physical challenges." He prayed out loud. "To at least be able to function well and take care of myself. To live on my own once Mom and Ted get married." He didn't even know when that would be. Hadn't asked because he was afraid it might be sometime soon. He sat there, eyes closed, at a loss for words, but certain God knew the heaviness wearing on him.

He finished the passage and placed the Bible back on his nightstand. Without dropping it.

It was at least an hour before Lexie would arrive. Mom was up, stirring around in the kitchen, starting breakfast.

It took just as much effort to get dressed as it usually did. But if he put in a hundred and ten percent on his recovery, God would bless his efforts.

Exhausted just from getting dressed, he started down the hall with his walker. Slow and steady, he managed to keep it quiet, to get to the therapy room with Mom none the wiser. He started on the balance ball. With both hands lightly on his walker, he did his best to stay steady. Admittedly, it was easier than the first time he'd tried it.

Next, he stood and walked to the parallel bars. By the time he heard Mom come down the hall, he'd been back and forth between them for an hour.

Her footsteps stopped at the therapy door instead of continuing on to his bedroom. "Clint, are you in there?"

"You can come in."

The door opened. Mom frowned. "What are you doing?"

"I thought I'd get an early start."

"How long have you been in here?" she asked.

"About an hour. I woke up early."

"Just don't wear yourself out." Her frown deepened.

"Don't worry. I'm determined, but I'm not looking to hurt myself."

But the pinch between her eyebrows stayed in place. "Breakfast is ready and Lexie should be here any minute."

"Thanks. On my way."

The doorbell rang.

"There she is," Mom announced, hurrying to get the door.

Clint made an effort not to clunk the walker. It made his progress slower, but he was so tired of the racket.

By the time he got to the table, Lexie was already

seated. She'd finally given up eating before she came in to appease his mom, who always had a plate for her.

"He's been up for an hour walking the parallel bars and using the balance ball. So do you think he's overdoing it?" Mom asked.

"Not at all," Lexie answered, smiling over at him. "You're steady enough on your feet now that you don't need me to be here in order to use the equipment. Feel free to work whenever you want. But if you start to feel tired or unsteady, take a break."

"But what if he falls?"

"I'll get up. Lexie showed me how."

"Patients who take the initiative on therapy recover faster." Lexie took a sip of her orange juice. "But no treadmill. We'll work on it next week and you're only allowed on it when someone is with you."

Was she as ready to be rid of him as he was her? Further proof that they had no future.

"Go fish, Uncle Clint." Cooper grinned, with every reason to. Seated at the kitchen table, he held three cards, while Clint still had five and none of them matched.

"Boy, would I like to go fishing." He drew a card. A five. No match, and he suspected Cooper held the other three since he'd consistently asked for a five for his last three turns.

"Me, too. Let's see if Lexie can go with us."

"Why Lexie?" Clint peered at his nephew over his cards.

"I like her. She's fun."

"Well, we already did our therapy for the day and she's gone home," he explained.

"I'm sure she'd come back if you call her."

"She probably would. But she needs time with her family, too. Maybe we can go fishing another day."

"Okay," Cooper agreed. "So do you have any fives?"

Clint closed his eyes, clutched his heart. "You're killing me, kid."

"Hand it over." Cooper giggled.

Clint handed his nephew the five.

"I win." Cooper let out a whoop and laid down all four fives.

"Again." Clint winced.

"I may have beat you, Uncle Clint, but you're not having as much trouble picking up cards and holding them as you used to."

"You're very observant," he remarked.

"Want to play catch?"

"Definitely. But see if Charlee can come."

"Okay." Cooper rolled his eyes. Obviously past his excitement of having a sister, he dashed out of the room.

"Whoa." Carly stepped aside just before Cooper crashed into her. "Slow down there."

"Sorry." Cooper flew past her.

"How long have you been there?"

"Long enough to see Cooper soundly beat you and to confirm he's still jealous of Charlee." She sighed. "I try to spend equal time with him, but it never seems to be enough. He needs his dad."

"He'll be home in just under two weeks."

"The longest thirteen days of my life." She sat down beside him. "You know I'm all about this country. All about being a military wife. But I'm ready for him to be home."

"Perfectly understandable." He reached his arm toward her.

She scooted her chair over beside him and leaned her head into his shoulder. "I've never worried so much in my life. Every night, I pray for his safety, give it over to God and go to sleep. And every morning, I take the worry back and it multiplies every minute throughout the day."

"God has kept him safe so far, we'll just have to continue to trust Him," Clint said, reassuringly. "How long will he get to stay home this time?"

"He's at the end of his active duty, so he'll have two years' inactive duty, take some college courses and—"

"Get some boring desk job."

"Some gloriously safe federal desk job," Carly retorted, smiling. "That is if he doesn't decide to enlist again."

"Barring that, you're almost home free."

"Hence the longest thirteen days of my life."

"I'm sorry I haven't been here for you through this." For not remembering how long Joel had been gone and when he was coming back.

"But you have been here. Through all of it. And if I have to explain everything twice, I'm okay with that. As long as you're here." She raised her face up to look at him, then shook her finger at him. "No more riding bulls. Do you hear me? Mom and I can't take any more of it."

"No more riding bulls."

"Even if you remember why you wanted to buy the ranch in Fort Worth and it's a really good reason."

"I promise," he assured her.

"I'll hold you to it." The corner of her mouth twitched.

"What do you think of Ted?"

"He's awesome, crazy about Mom, and he's really good to her," Carly answered softly. "After Dad, I didn't think she'd ever be truly happy again. But Ted makes her happy."

"No red flags?"

"None."

"I found it!" Cooper blasted through the door, holding a volleyball.

"I was hoping for a baseball." Clint stood. "Let me see if I can find one."

"Grandma said you have to sit down while we play and

a baseball will hurt you if you don't catch it. She said you wouldn't like it, but you can lump it."

"Sounds like Grandma." Clint chuckled. "Okay, for now. But we're gonna play baseball soon."

"Okay. Come on." Cooper bolted for the door.

Focus, get stronger, more mobile and active. Even with Dad's downhill trajectory, he'd learned to be self-sufficient. Until the end. Clint had the same therapist. He had to beat this. As much as he could.

He clunked his way to the living room. Mom sat on the couch with some sort of catalog in her lap. She closed it and set it aside.

"Be careful. Do you hear me?"

"It's a volleyball. I'm pretty sure I'll be okay."

"I just worry about you."

"I'm fine." He shot her a wink. "And I approve of Ted."

"You do?" She looked up at him, teary-eyed.

He nodded. "Invite him over whenever you want."

"Oh, Clint." Mom got up, standing on tiptoe to hug him. "I'm so glad you like him." Her words came out soggy.

But they were happy tears. And that was all he wanted, for his mom to be happy. If Ted did that for her, he'd just have to get used to the guy being around.

Chapter Ten

"You're rocking the parallel bars lately." Lexie watched Clint's progress. He didn't even bobble anymore.

"I've been walking this cattle chute a lot in the mornings before you get here and in the evenings after you leave."

"I can tell. Just don't overdo it and exhaust yourself. Any more memories?"

"No." Disappointment echoed through the single word.

"But you had a memory the other night. That means more will follow."

"Out of all the pivotal things that have happened in the last two years—the birth of my niece, my brother-in-law getting sent to Afghanistan, my mom getting engaged—I remember something insignificant like a radio preacher I like."

"Good Biblical preaching is never insignificant. And it tells you a lot about yourself. That you like church, you hate missing the services and you enjoy fiery preaching."

"I already knew all of that." Frustration dripped from his tone. "Maybe I could leave my walker here when we go outside today."

"Not just yet. Walking on uneven ground is a whole different animal. But soon."

"I'm ready to go when you are." He navigated the remainder of the bars, then transferred to his walker.

"We need to do the balance ball."

"Later. I'm tired of being cooped up." He headed for the door.

"All righty then. I can see we're not going to get anywhere in here." She followed as he went down the hall.

But he stopped at the end. "Morning, Ted." He sounded strained, obviously still struggling with his mother's engagement.

"Morning. You're looking chipper."

"I was," Clint muttered under his breath, then stepped into the kitchen.

"Hello, Lexie," Ted greeted her.

"Hey, Mom, Lexie and I were about to go check on the cattle. Do you mind if Ted goes with me today instead of Lexie?"

Audrey's eyebrows went up. "I, um—"

"I'll play nice," Clint promised.

"I'd love to come with you," Ted said. "Always been curious about beefalo."

"Great, I'll show you around and the ladies can visit. That okay with you, Lexie?"

"Of course."

"You could hang on to my arm and ditch the walker if you want?" Ted offered his arm.

"I'm good." Clint trudged toward the kitchen door.

So far Ted rated worse than the walker. She hoped this walk went well. Audrey really needed the two men in her life to bond.

Ted held the door open until Clint made it through, then winked at Audrey and followed.

As soon as the door shut behind them, Audrey moved to the window. "What do you think that's about?"

"I'm not sure. Should I have gone with them?"

"No. Clint told me last night that he approves of Ted, so they should be okay by themselves." She blew out a breath. "Poor Ted. Not many men would be patient enough to go through the meet-and-win-over-the-son thing twice."

"He's crazy about you."

Audrey smiled. "I'm crazy about him."

"Good thing, too, since the wedding is in exactly a month."

"I hope Clint is back to normal by then. Ted thinks we should postpone it. Until my boy fully recovers."

"You've still got time to decide on that." She joined Audrey to peer out the window.

Ted supported Clint's walker as he slowly made it down each step. What would they talk about? Would conversation be stiff and stilted between them? Or would Clint grill Ted, give him the third degree? She hoped not. From her vantage point, the Rawlins family needed Ted. Levi's death had left a gaping hole in the fabric of their family and Ted seemed like just the man to mend it.

"So what do you like most about my mom?" Clint started things off with the most pressing thing on his mind.

Ted's eyes softened. "Her kindness, gentleness and her smile."

"What brought you to Medina?"

"My sister and her husband were tired of the hustle and bustle of living in San Antonio, so they bought a weekend home in Medina. I visited them here and fell in love with the peaceful atmosphere."

"Do you mind if I ask what your wife was like?"

"Worried I'm trying to find a carbon copy in your mom?" Ted dug his wallet out. "I can assure you that's not the case." He showed Clint a picture of a red-haired woman. Freckles and dark eyes. Tiny stature.

Nothing like Mom physically.

"Maryann was vivacious, the life of the party. She lived large and loud, was into raising money for charities, and bungee jumping."

Worlds apart from Mom's personality. Though she'd probably like the charity thing since she had a big heart for people in need.

"I loved her dearly, but I'm more of an introvert. Sometimes Maryann wore me out as I tried to keep up with her. Your mom has a soothing, peaceful presence." Ted put the picture back in his wallet and stuffed it in his pocket. "Can I ask you a few questions now?"

"I may not know the answer, but I'll try."

"You'll know this one. What was your dad like? I've tried to get your mom to open up about him, but she thinks we shouldn't spend a lot of time talking about the past. That we should just move on with the future."

"It sounds like he was a lot like your wife." Clint's heart clenched, as he stared at white puffy clouds in the distance, missing Dad something awful. "He loved the rodeo and was always looking for adventure and excitement. Mom refused to go bungee jumping, but he always wanted to try it. Staying home wasn't on his agenda.

"When Carly and I were young, we camped along the rodeo circuit during the summers. He was always taking us places between rodeos, *experiencing life* as he called it. Mom is more like you, I think. She'd have liked to just stay home most of the time." While Clint had dreaded having to go back to school again when the summer ended and the adventure was over.

"So your mother and I married opposites, and now we've found each other and learned we're a lot alike. Peaceful homebodies."

"You'll be good to her?"

"I plan to spend the rest of my life doing my very best to keep her happy."

Clint looked over at him. "I can't ask for any more than that."

"I hope you'll stick around here. She was dreading you moving to Fort Worth. And I know it's none of my business, but she needs for you to quit the rodeo," Ted said firmly.

"I appreciate your concern." Clint turned his walker toward the barn. "I have no idea why I wanted to move or why I thought the rodeo was the only way I could do it." Had he seen the Fort Worth ranch as an adventure? "But bull riding was never my thing like it was for Dad. I only resorted to it for cash. And I've learned it's not something you want to do sporadically if you want to stay in one piece."

"Smart man." Moos and grunts echoed from the field. "The moos almost sound like those of a regular cow," Ted commented.

"They're 3/8 bison and 5/8 bovine, so it makes sense for them to moo, but you should hear the bulls in mating season. They almost sound like donkeys."

"You've got a fine operation here, son." Ted patted him on the back.

"Have I never shown them to you before?"

Ted hung his head. "It's been a while and I wanted to spend some time with you."

"Did we do that before? Spend time together?"

"Some. I always enjoyed it," Ted admitted.

His heart tugged. "But I never told you why I wanted to buy the ranch in Fort Worth?"

"No."

But there was something in the older man's eyes. Like he knew something he wasn't telling.

"You know something, don't you?"

"I have a theory. But Lexie said we should keep our theories to ourselves, let you sort things out on your own."

"Can't you give me a hint?"

Ted chuckled. "Afraid not. 'Cause if I'm wrong, then you'll be thinking something you never thought."

"Fair enough." His walker knocked against a rock.

"Don't they make better walkers these days, that scoot along instead of being so unwieldy?"

"Yes. But Lexie says they won't give me enough stability. It's not heavy, just noisy."

"Then I reckon we better listen. That little lady knows her stuff." Ted walked at a snail's pace, staying right with Clint.

"I just wish I could remember why I was so desperate for money. I didn't get into anything stupid, like gambling or anything, did I?" He squeezed his eyes closed.

"Not that I know of. It doesn't seem like your character and I sincerely doubt you were into anything shady or illegal." Ted clapped him on the back. "Maybe you just saw a good opportunity to expand. Your mom said online direct to consumer sales are up this year. I can't believe there's not some grocery store or distributor out there ready to get in on your business."

Something flickered in Clint's mind. But he couldn't put his finger on it. They reached the barn and his prize bull strolled by.

"I tell you what, if you remember why you wanted to expand to Fort Worth and the place is still up for sale, I'd be interested in putting the cash up for you. We could be partners."

"That's kind of you. But the owner had other buyers interested. It's probably already gone."

"I'm not trying to be kind. It's business." Ted sounded sincere, and he was clearly not trying to throw his money around to buy Clint's loyalty. On the contrary, he seemed genuinely interested in the beefalo business and it really meant a lot to Clint. "Your mom told me all about how you saved the ranch a few years ago. She's right proud of you."

"I couldn't let her lose the ranch. Not after Dad rode all those bulls to buy it, so she'd have somewhere to be a homebody when he retired." But she'd ended up without Dad. The loss put a pang in his heart.

"So that's why she's so stuck on living here after we're married."

"She is?" The perfect opportunity to ask about the date. But he was still getting used to everything. He didn't need a timeline.

"Says it's because she doesn't want anybody to think she's marrying me for my money. I'm renting right now, but I want to build your mom a house. I sold the home Maryann and I built in San Antonio. Most people don't need twenty-three bedrooms, but I wanted it to be big enough to accommodate her family reunions. It did and then some, but it was so big it never felt like home to us."

"Yeah, Mom would hate living somewhere like that."

Ted nodded. "Just something big enough to have Thanksgiving and Christmas dinner gatherings and a few overnight guests, but still cozy is what I'd like."

"Maybe she'll agree after a few years." He couldn't believe he was standing here talking about Mom getting married. Being someone else's wife.

"I'd like to deed the ranch over to you since Carly and Joel don't have any interest in it. Then to be fair to them, I'd pay them the fair market value of the place."

"That's way too generous of you." Clint had a decent balance in his account, but he couldn't imagine being able to make an offer like that. "I'm not sure we could accept."

"Now you sound like your mom," Ted mumbled, adjusting his hat. "I know there are a lot of changes for you right now, but I'd like to be a good one. I don't think there's any law against us hanging out, is there? And I always felt like we could be close if we had the time."

Ted was a good man and Clint needed Mom to be okay if his mental health took a wrong turn. Ted would see that she was.

"I try to walk about this time every day. Keeps me from feeling cooped up."

"I'll make a point to be here part of the time. I don't want to crowd you."

Clint stopped, offering his hand.

Ted clasped it. Solid grip.

"I'm okay with you coming round to see Mom."

Kind, blue eyes went misty. "Thank you. You have no idea what that means to me." Ted hugged him.

"It means a lot to me that you care that I approve of your relationship with Mom. And that you've had the patience to strive for it twice."

"You mean the world to her and she means the world to me." Ted clapped him on the back, then let go. "You know Maryann and I never had any kids, so I kind of feel like this is my second chance at that, too. I mean, not to replace your dad, I'd never try to do that. But I want us to be family."

Clint nodded, not sure he could say anything around the lump in his throat. Ted seemed like a really great guy. But he'd give anything if he could have his dad back.

"Now, show me those beefalo." Ted offered his arm. "Ready to ditch the walker yet?"

It was one thing hanging on to Lexie. She was his therapist and he trusted her because she'd worked with Dad. Hanging on to Ted would make him seem weak.

"Leaning, leaning, leaning on the everlasting arms." Ted's rich baritone soothed. "Now I'm not claiming to be God, but I am a Christian and sometimes He provides someone to give you a strong arm when you need it. I just think you'd be steadier out here if you weren't having to work the walker and your feet."

Clint took a deep breath, then placed his hand on Ted's arm. The older man patted his hand and they headed for the barn.

And sure enough, with Ted's support, each step came easier.

"I love jigsaw puzzles." Lexie's fingers itched to put pieces into place.

"I'm glad you're enjoying this."

And Clint itched to be outside.

She'd actually missed him yesterday, since his mom wasn't as nervous about him staying home while she'd gone to church and then eaten at Old Spanish Trail. The entire day without him had been long and lonely. A very bad sign.

"Did you notice I came dressed for the occasion?" She'd worn her favorite scrubs, black with neon puzzle pieces everywhere.

"As soon as you walked in this morning, I knew the agenda for the day." Clint slipped a piece into place, forming part of a palomino horse's face.

"We can take the puzzle outside if you'd like."

"I'd rather be outside doing something physical. I'm good with puzzles. We used to do them as a family in the winter months when I was a kid. But I feel so useless sitting around all the time."

"This is the first time you've sat down today. And puzzles are very good therapy. There's a lot of reasoning that goes into putting them together."

"Do you think I could go for a horseback ride?" He looked so hopeful. Almost childlike.

She couldn't burst his bubble. Even though he really needed to work on cognitive and fine motor skills. "You won't believe this, but since I gave horseback riding lessons to help pay for college, I ended up getting certified as an equine therapist."

His smile came from within and threatened to light up the room. "Aren't you just full of surprises."

"Were you a good rider before your accident?"

"Excellent," he admitted.

"Do you have a really gentle horse? One that doesn't spook. No matter what."

"Yes. But I've fallen off a horse before. And I got right back on."

"You're recovering from a brain injury, Clint. We don't need another knock to your noggin. Are there any helmets on the ranch?"

"There are some in the barn. Mom used to give riding lessons when Carly and I were in high school."

"As good as you've gotten with the balance ball, I think a horseback ride is a good idea. *If* you can find a helmet. And no going alone when I'm not here."

"Scout's honor."

The two of them alone. For hours. Her heart skipped a beat at the prospect.

Stop it.

"Ever seen a beefalo calf?"

"I'd never seen a beefalo until I came here."

He flashed her an infectious grin. "That's about to change. But first, let's see about getting you some boots."

"I actually have some in my car." She slipped a piece of the puzzle in place. "I keep a change of clothes in case I need to go somewhere after work. I hate wearing scrubs in public. They defeat all sense of fashion."

"You manage to say a lot with scrubs. Will you have to go back to a certain solid color when you start your new job?"

"Thankfully, no. The clinic doesn't care as long as we

wear scrubs. I'll go get my clothes." She scurried out of the room.

"Leaving already?" Audrey asked as Lexie cut past to the foyer.

She stopped, popping her head in the living room. "I have clothes and boots in my car, so I'm gonna change real quick, then take Clint on a horseback ride."

Audrey's eyes widened. "Can he handle that?"

"I'm a certified equine therapist. He's been really working the balance ball and the parallel bars. I wouldn't take him if I was worried he might fall off and I'm making him wear a helmet. Want to join us?"

"No, I'd be a nervous wreck. Y'all go and have fun. But be careful."

Why had she agreed to go horseback riding with him? *Oh, yeah, that's right. Because surely it would be better than being cooped up in the same room with Mr. Way-Too-Cute Cowboy.*

In the car, she sorted through her extra clothes. Jeans and boots, a casual T-shirt that didn't seem right for riding horses, a pink plaid button-up and a rhinestone-spattered turquoise tee. She chose the last and hurried back inside.

Chapter Eleven

Clint tapped his foot.

"Are you sure you can ride?" Mom asked for the umpteenth time.

"I'm positive. And besides, doctors frequently prescribe equine therapy for patients with balance issues, and Lexie is fully certified."

"If you fall off, I'll kill you." Audrey jabbed a finger at him.

"Lexie's trying to make me wear a helmet."

"I knew I liked Lexie. She's a smart girl."

Footfalls sounded in the hallway.

As she stepped into the living room, her pale blue-green long-sleeved top flashed rhinestones. She'd paired it with jeans with spangled pockets and cowgirl boots. He had to fight to keep his jaw from dropping. He'd seen her in scrubs and casual clothing, but never cowgirl gear. She looked like something out of a magazine.

"Thought you might need this." He held a cowgirl hat toward her. "It's Carly's. Keep you from getting a sunburn."

"Thanks." She plopped the hat in place.

"Ready?"

She nodded. "We still have to find that helmet."

"I was hoping you'd forget."

"Clint Rawlins, you're not leaving this house unless you promise to wear a helmet," his mom admonished.

"I won't let him ride unless he does." Lexie propped her hands on her hips. "And since we're going outside, you'll have to use the walker."

"After you." Clint stepped aside to let her pass. Coconut perfume wafted over him as she slipped her blue jean jacket on. Maybe if he stayed downwind from Lexie, looking at the beefalo instead of her, his heart would survive this ride intact.

He followed her outside and they slowly made their way to the barn.

"So which stall is the helmet in?"

"All the tack and saddles are in the first stall. Mom asked one of the hands to get two horses ready for us. Her saddle should fit you."

"Calm horses, right?"

"You're not afraid of horses, too, are you?"

"No. Just cows. I can handle a wild steed, but your noggin can't."

He stepped into the first stall. Two helmets hung on the wall. He chose the larger one.

"Here we are." He set it on his head, stepped out of the stall and leaned against it so he could secure the strap under his chin with both hands. But his fingers fumbled. It should be simple, click in place like Cooper's old car seat. Maybe if he had a mirror…

"Let me." She stepped close, placed her hands on each side of the helmet, testing the fit. Then adjusted the dial on the side, making it fit better. "That okay?"

"Yes." Except for her proximity stealing his breath.

She adjusted the strap under his chin and clicked it in place. "There. All set. Want me to wear one, too?"

"That's up to you."

"Here you go, Mr. Rawlins." A ranch hand he didn't recognize led two Sorrels toward them.

"Thanks." Try as he might, Clint couldn't come up with a name. Must be new.

He took the reins of one mare, while Lexie took the other. The hand tipped his hat, then left them alone.

"Once you get on the horse, you don't get to take off. I want to make sure you can balance first."

"Yes, ma'am."

"Think you can manage getting up there on your own?"

"I've done it my whole life." He leaned against the mare, lifted his left foot and stepped into the stirrup. While holding the reins, he gripped the saddle with his left hand, and then with a little jump, he hauled himself up. Felt a little teeter, but managed to cling to the saddle horn, regain his balance and throw his right leg over the horse's back. His right foot slipped into the stirrup.

It might not have been pretty or smooth, but he'd made it. And he was holding his balance pretty well.

"You're doing well sitting. Can you stand in the stirrups?"

He drew in a deep breath, pushed himself up, wobbled a bit. But not much.

"I think you can do this."

"Me, too. Let's go."

She gave him a pointed look. "Just walking, okay?"

"Yes, ma'am."

They reined their horses out of the barn. Behind the structure, the hand waited at the gate and swung it open for them.

"Thanks." No name again.

"Have a good ride." The hand latched the gate behind them.

In the open pasture, they rode side by side. Wide open spaces surrounded him. He could breathe better out here and riding gave him the ability to move freely without having to coordinate his awkward limbs. He missed that. Walking without thinking. Picking up something without thinking. Fastening a latch without thinking.

"Are you taking me in the middle of the herd?"

"Maybe. Depends on where they are," he answered.

"I'm afraid of cows and you're taking me in the middle of a herd of beefalo."

"They're docile, probably won't pay us any mind." He breathed in the scent of hay, horse and fresh air. Wildflowers dotted the path, mostly bluebonnets and crimson Indian paintbrush.

"Are the mothers protective like cows?" Her voice caught.

"Don't worry. I won't take you too close to the calf."

"My mom and dad were riding a four-wheeler once, with me behind them on another. We got too close to a longhorn mama and she came after me. I was screaming, but with the noise of our engines, they didn't know anything was going on. We were on a narrow path and I nearly rammed the rear end of their four-wheeler trying to get away from her. I felt the shadow of her horns, but I guess we got far enough away, she was happy again and left me alone."

Clint chuckled. "So you've been chased by a cow three times, then?"

"I guess I blocked this one from my memory. It was by far the scariest because of the mile-long horns."

"I'm sure. Did your parents take the cow's side that time, too?"

"Yep, they said I got too close to her baby."

"There they are." He gestured off in the distance where the herd gathered in the middle of an open field. The new mama, with the calf lying down, hung at the edge.

"Please don't take me too close."

"I won't. Trust me."

She fell silent as they neared the herd. Her tension echoed between them.

"It looks like a regular calf," she whispered. "Where's the hump and the curly forehead?"

"They're 17 to 37.5 percent bison blood. Some of them just look like muscled-up cows." He stopped his horse, close enough to see the cream-colored calf, but far enough away to keep the wary-eyed mother calm. Yet the calf didn't move. "I think he might be sick. Or injured."

"What can we do?"

"Well, normally, I'd call some of the hands and then sweet-talk the mama while the hands cut her off from the calf before she knew what was happening. I'd see if she'd put up with me picking her calf up, putting him on my horse and taking him back to the barn." Frustration oozed through him at not being able to do what had to be done.

"There's no way I'm letting you get down to even see about it. You don't need to end up trying to outrun a mad mama beefalo."

"I'll call the hands, let them handle it." He slipped his phone out of his pocket. But he didn't know any of their names or numbers. Probably all in his phone, but he wouldn't recognize the names.

He'd have to ring the house and get Mom to call a hand. He dialed the number. His mother answered on the third ring.

"Hey, Mom, I'm with the herd in the south pasture. I think the new calf is sick."

"Oh dear, I'll send some of the hands. How's the ride?"

"Really good. I didn't have any trouble."

"I'm glad, sweetheart. You always loved to ride."

"See you back at the house in a bit." He hung up, peered at the calf, then closed his eyes.

"You'll get there." Lexie leaned forward, stroking her

horse's shoulder. "One day, you'll be able to take on a mama beefalo. But even then, I hope you won't do it without backup."

He turned and saw four ranch hands riding in the distance. "We'll stay until they can see where the calf is, then head back. She might get combative and I don't want to freak you out."

"And I don't want you falling off your horse on my watch."

Once the men got close enough, he realized the one in front was Ted. He waved, motioned to where the calf lay, and then headed back toward the ranch house.

Ted was taking his place. But he couldn't think about it that way. Ted hadn't had to come; he could have let the hands take care of the calf. But he'd been at the house, and when Mom had told him what was going on, he must've decided to ride there with the hands. Mom needed that. A man willing to help when he wasn't required to.

But no matter what Lexie said, Clint felt like a failure. He couldn't even tend to his cattle. What business did he have thinking about how good she smelled? Or looked. Once again, he reminded himself, he was in no shape to begin a relationship.

"You're doing great with your balance. Barely even holding on," Lexie said encouragingly.

Clint's phone chimed. He held on to one of the parallel bars, then slipped his phone from his pocket, swiped the screen and focused on it. "So the hands gave the calf penicillin yesterday and he's up walking around now."

"I'm so glad. Poor little fella. I'm glad we went out riding when we did."

"The hands would have checked on him before it got dark, but I guess we spared him some suffering."

Lexie stepped back until she was a good five feet from

the end of the parallel bars. "See if you can walk to me. Without your walker."

"You really think I can?"

"We won't know until you try."

Clint took a big breath. "Here goes nothing." He stepped out of the cattle chute, as he liked to call it, and took a cautious step toward her. No bobble or swaying. His smile went all the way to his eyes.

"Come on." She motioned him toward her with both hands. "But don't get in a hurry."

Another hesitant step, then a series of several. Coming too fast.

"Not so fast. Take your time."

But it was too late—he was already careening to the left.

She caught him with a hand on each of his biceps, helped him regain his balance. His arms came around her shoulders. Way too close.

"Sorry about that. I didn't mean to fall for you." His gaze caught hers, then dipped to her lips.

The door opened and Cooper stepped inside. "Why are you hugging Lexie, Uncle Clint? Is she your girlfriend now?"

"No." Lexie stepped back, setting the walker in front of him. "We were seeing how well he could walk. I had to support him a little."

Carly hurried into the room. "I'm so sorry. Cooper, you're supposed to knock and I told you to leave Uncle Clint alone until he finishes his therapy for the day."

"I was afraid we'd have to leave without seeing him. We have to go because I have homework and if I stay caught up all week, we get to go to the rodeo Friday night. But I'm not supposed to say anything because rodeo is a touchy subject around here."

"Cooper!" Carly reprimanded.

"It's okay, you can go to the rodeo. I hope you have fun and it won't bother me." Clint grinned, but there was a hint of sadness in his eyes.

Did he miss it? Was he longing to go back to the sport that could kill him? All the more reason to keep her distance.

"I don't see why you can't go, Uncle Clint. You can sit on the bottom bleacher with the old people who can't climb the stands."

"Cooper, please stop talking." Carly closed her eyes, gave a tiny shake of her head. "Give your uncle a hug and let's let him get back to work."

"Bye, Uncle Clint. I love you." Cooper hugged Clint's middle.

"I love you, too, my main man." Clint's eyes went glossy.

Carly gave him a quick hug and hustled her son out of the room.

"There's a rodeo in Medina?" Clint asked, swiping at his eyes.

Lexie nodded. "My friend Larae started it on her ranch last year. It was outdoor at first, but she opened an indoor facility last summer."

"Is it professionally sanctioned?"

"Yes."

"Year round?"

"Yes." Interest lit Clint's eyes. Maybe he wouldn't have to travel the circuit. He could get his kicks every weekend right down the road. And he was obviously raring to go.

"I wonder why I didn't compete there instead of San Antonio?" he mused.

"The purse is probably bigger in San Antonio, though I think Larae's rodeo is getting to be a pretty big deal."

"Why can't I go?"

So he *was* missing it. "Dr. Arnett thought going places

with a lot of people who know you but you don't remember might be overwhelming."

"But it could jog my memory," Clint countered.

"I guess it could."

He exhaled roughly. "I've come to terms with my situation, Lexie. Weeks have passed since I woke up in the hospital. I think I can handle going to the rodeo with my nephew without freaking out."

"Tell you what. You work on the balance ball some more, while I go see what your mom thinks. If she's game, I'll check with Dr. Arnett. But you'll have to take your walker."

"Deal." He clunked the walker to the ball, settled on it all by himself. "And I think I've earned myself another horseback ride. Maybe tomorrow."

The ball tilted and he adjusted his weight, only for it to twist the other direction. No matter what he did, it swayed one way or the other. But at least he could manage the hoppity-hop, as he called it, without it flipping him into the floor now.

"You're riding that thing like a pro. And, sure, we could go riding again sometime." She forced a smile. "I'll be right back." She stepped out of the room, shut the door and inhaled deeply.

If Cooper hadn't interrupted, would Clint have kissed her? Would she have let him?

This could *not* happen. Though his physical condition had greatly improved, he obviously missed the rodeo. And his mental capacity was still off-kilter. She had to keep it professional, finish this job and escape Clint Rawlins.

Chapter Twelve

Clint focused on the parallel bars. Not on Lexie. "So it's treadmill time."

"I think you're up to it."

"Here goes nothing." He thudded his walker over to the only piece of equipment he hadn't used yet.

She steadied him while he stepped onto the mat. "Now hold on to the bars and put your feet all the way to the edge on each side, off the track that moves."

He followed her instructions.

"Clip this cord to the hem of your shirt and if you get too far back, the safety key will pull out and automatically kill the engine."

"Okay." He managed the clip by himself.

"Now, once I turn it on, don't step on the track until you've watched it for a bit, feel the rhythm of it and how fast you'll have to walk. Here we go." She turned the motor on and the mat inched along under him.

"Really? That slow?"

"To begin with. Yes."

He watched the mat, felt the cadence, stepped on with one foot, then slid backward before he could move his other foot. The cord clipped to his shirt tightened until the key pulled out. The track stopped.

"See, it's faster than it seems. But you'll get it." She waited for him to step off onto the edge, then started the machine again.

He managed to get both feet on the mat, on the second try. It took all his concentration to keep up. Much harder than he thought.

"Very good," Lexie said, turning the treadmill off.

"That's all? That was like maybe two minutes."

"But it took a lot out of you, didn't it?"

His breathing came fast. "Maybe."

"Our time's pretty much up for the day anyway. We'll do some more tomorrow." She helped him safely off the torture rack. "And absolutely no trying the treadmill without having someone right here with you. Do I need to take the key home to make certain of that?"

"Nope. I get it. It's a lot harder than I thought and I have no desire to get wrapped around it like some cartoon character."

"Good. My job here is done."

He caught her gaze. "Can you stay for an early supper?"

"I don't know… I should probably go on home." She checked her watch. "It's Wednesday and I usually go to Bible study."

"Exactly why Mom scheduled it early, so we could go. Ted's coming, along with Carly and the kids. I'm going to officially give him and Mom my blessing. I could use your support."

Her eyes softened. "I'm glad. And proud of you. Sure, I'll stay for that."

"Thanks." He walked across the room without his walker, managing to stay steady.

"Very good. You'll be walking on your own before you know it."

"Confession, I didn't use it in the house last night after you left."

"I'm impressed," she said, before checking her watch again. "What time is supper?"

"Five thirty."

"I have a change of clothes in my car as usual."

"I assumed. You can use my bathroom." He settled on the balance ball.

"Thanks," she murmured, hurrying out of the room.

His movements were almost back to normal and he rarely got off balance. Last night, he'd played pitch with Cooper and hadn't had any trouble throwing or catching the baseball. All of the seemingly insignificant board and card games he'd played with Lexie and Cooper over the last few weeks had retrained his brain. He could walk, eat, dress and clean up after himself.

But except for recalling the radio preacher, his memory was just as blank as it had been when he'd woken up in the hospital.

Voices in the kitchen meant Lexie was finished in his bathroom.

He walked inside, cleaned up, sprayed fresh cologne and changed into jeans and a button-up shirt. He could even manage the buttons. But his time with his pretty therapist was more than half over. And that made him sad.

But he had no business thinking about dating her. He couldn't sentence her or anyone else to the degenerative disease that had killed Dad.

He splashed water on his face and headed for the kitchen.

While Mom added spices to something bubbling on the stove, Lexie set the table. Her red top and jeans seemed out of place, since he was used to seeing her dressed in scrubs. But no matter what she wore, she was a knockout.

"Can I do anything to help?" he offered, as the doorbell rang. "That'll be Ted. I'll get it." He strolled to the foyer and opened the door.

Ted came in carrying Charlee, with Cooper holding his hand. Carly was still in the car.

"We found Grandpa." Charlee giggled.

"I see that." Charlee had never known her real Grandpa. Clint stepped aside so they could enter.

"They asked if they could call me that once we announced the engagement. Hope you're okay with it."

"It's fine." But the words tasted bitter.

"Mommy got a call from work, but she's coming in a minute," Cooper reported.

"Okay, Monkey. Let me set you down so I can go help your Grandma."

Monkey. Charlee climbing his leg. Like a monkey. "Did I give her that nickname?"

"You said she should be in a zoo." Cooper snickered.

"I remember." Clint tried to come up with more details. Nothing.

"That's wonderful." Ted clapped him on the back. "See, it's coming to you. Slowly, but surely."

He almost got teary. Not only had he remembered coming up with the nickname, he'd remembered Charlee. It was definitely a slow process and he could only hope on the surely part.

The door whooshed open and Carly scurried inside. "Sorry about that. I had to talk the new loan clerk at work through a computer program."

"Everything's ready," Mom called from the kitchen.

"I timed that just right, didn't I?" Carly grabbed Charlee and steered her toward the kitchen. "Come on, Cooper." Ted and Clint followed.

"Look what the stray cat dragged in," Clint quipped as he entered the kitchen.

Ted roared with laughter.

"Y'all sit." Mom rolled her eyes with a good-natured grin.

He genuinely liked Ted and appreciated his sense of

humor, and the man was good to Mom. The only thing was—he just wasn't Dad.

Everyone stood around the table. With six chairs and one holding Charlee's booster seat, someone would have to sit in Dad's chair.

"Why don't you sit at the head of the table, Clint?" Mom gestured him there.

He didn't feel worthy, but he didn't want Ted sitting there. With a sense of reverence, he sank into the chair with Lexie to his right, as everyone else claimed their seats.

Mom ladled heaping mounds of chicken and dumplings into each bowl. "This is one of Clint's favorite meals. And Ted's, as well. Y'all actually have a lot in common."

"Mainly, that we both love you," Clint summed up. "And about that, I want to officially give your relationship my blessing."

Mom clasped a hand to her heart and turned glossy eyes on him. "Thank you, son. You have no idea how much that means to me."

"I'm sure there aren't a lot of men who have acquired the approval of their sweetheart's son twice." Clint chuckled. "Thanks for your patience, Ted."

"I'm right honored." Ted's jaw developed a tick; the man was obviously keeping a tight rein on his emotions.

A hand touched his under the table. Lexie? He turned to face her and she gave him an approving smile. Her fingers twined with his and she squeezed his hand. He could get used to that. But she was only trying to support him. If only she could be his lifetime support.

The calf was nursing. It was so cute it almost made Lexie teary-eyed. Yes, the calf would grow into a huge creature she'd be afraid of someday, but right now it was adorable.

"Thanks for putting therapy off a bit for this ride. I

needed it." Clint stared at a row of huge round hay bales lining the fence.

"You deserved a reward after dinner last night. You made two people very happy."

"Mom deserves happiness. I couldn't stand in the way of it." He pointed toward the bales. "I used to climb up there and watch the herd for hours. There's something peaceful, relaxing about it."

Morning dew glistened on the bales still in the shade. But the heat of the sun had dried the ones farther from the fence row.

"Let's ride over there."

"Why?" he queried.

"Because I think you can climb up there."

"I don't think so."

"Come on." She gave a slight snap of reins, then aimed her horse toward the bales. "I'll help you."

"You got a ladder hidden on your horse?"

"Oh, stop! You don't need a ladder."

"Whatever you say," he muttered.

They reached the bales and she dismounted, hovered nearby as he did. Slightly wobbly, but remarkable compared to where he'd been a few weeks ago.

A patch of cactus caught her attention. The green pads shaped like thick Ping-Pong paddles lined with tufts of needles.

"Watch for prickly pears. They can trip you up and you don't want to fall and land on one." She held on to his arm as they slowly walked over to the bales. "Lean on me if you need to. You're really doing amazing, Clint."

"I don't feel amazing."

"A few weeks ago, you couldn't feed yourself. Or get on the balance ball by yourself."

He blew out a breath. "I know, but all of that seems insignificant when it comes to daily life."

"You'll get your life back. All of it."

"I hope so. This invalid thing is getting old," he harrumphed. "I know I should be thankful. There are people who've suffered way more than I have and are way worse off than me."

"Illness or physical challenges are always hardest on the self-sufficient male." They stopped in front of the smallest round bale. "Okay, up we go."

She dug the toe of her boot into the end of the bale, jumped with her other foot, grabbed the twine holding the bale together and pulled herself up. Then plopped down and turned to face him. Straddling the bale, she held her hand out to him.

"I'll look like a whale thrashing about."

"There's no way to climb a hay bale gracefully. Nobody's watching but me and I'm not concerned with what you look like." She shouldn't be, anyway. If only he weren't so handsome. "I just don't want you to fall."

He sank the toe of his boot into the bale and found a good foothold.

"Give me your hand."

He grabbed on to her and made his way up, with very little bobbling.

"I knew you could do it!"

"Did I look like a whale?" he asked.

"Not at all." She held his hands and helped him stand.

He wobbled, but she wrapped her arms around his waist, managing to steady him. With her face in his chest, his arms around her shoulders, her heart clamored. She should take a step back. But oh, how she didn't want to. He was warm and so terribly strong and male.

She forced her feet back, letting go of him. "You okay?"

When he swayed again, she grabbed his hands. He found his balance, but she didn't let go.

"I used to jump from bale to bale at Larae's ranch, with

her and Stacia when we were kids. There'd be a couple of feet between them sometimes." She shook her head. "The things we used to do as kids. Gives me the shudders now. Like jumping out of the barn loft. Everything was bigger when I was a kid, but it didn't seem so high up then. It's a wonder we never broke a leg. Or our necks."

"Dad and I used to come out here. Watch the herd and then the sunset." His gaze left hers, went to the sky. "Until he got to where he couldn't climb the bales. It was hard on him. Hard for me to watch. What if I end up like him?"

"You're progressing in the opposite direction. You just got to where you can climb the bales. It'll only get better from here."

"I hope so." His words came out thick. "But right now, I can't even take care of my herd or my business."

"I know it's frustrating. But you'll get there. You remind me of him."

His gaze met hers again. "My hands are meeting with a beefalo breeder today."

"Selling off stock, investing in more. I'm guessing you can't find beefalo at the weekly sale barn."

"No, but how do you know about the sale barn?"

"My dad's been a ranch foreman my entire life. I've even gone with him to the sale barn," she confided. "He used to let me pick cows to buy, said I was better at it than him. They don't scare me at all when they're in nice pens and stock trailers."

"I grew up going with Dad and he used to let me pick stock. Normally, I'd be in the big middle of it, making all the decisions alone now. But I don't trust my judgment right now. This time, my ranch hands went in my place. I don't even know their names."

"You'll get there."

"Thank you for getting me this far. For listening to me whine."

"No problem." She smiled. "You're far from the whiniest I've had."

His gaze dropped to her mouth.

Everything in her wanted to lean in. But she couldn't. She was certain he'd recover fully physically. But mentally, was he capable of really knowing if he wanted to kiss her? Or was it the classic therapist-patient scenario where emotions got tangled with gratitude? And then there was the rodeo thing…

She took a step back. "We better get you home so we don't wear you out." She sat down on the bale, scooted her way down the side of it and jumped. "Besides, that jigsaw puzzle's not gonna do itself."

"I was hoping that puzzle would go away," he grumbled.

"Tell you what, if you work on the puzzle, we'll work on the treadmill this afternoon."

He quirked a brow. "Resorting to bribery, are we?"

"And you get to go to the rodeo this weekend."

"You win." He waved her back. "I doubt my dismount will be pretty. You can't stand there and take the chance of me creaming you."

"Don't try to jump. It's not far and there's a cushion of loose hay here. Just slide down the side and don't worry about landing on your feet so much."

"Sink or swim." He slid down and somehow landed on his feet.

As he started to totter, she grabbed his hands and steadied him.

"You've got hay in your hair." He reached behind her, grazing her ear with his finger.

Which sent a shiver coursing through her. "Let's get you on your horse." She turned away, then stood near as he mounted. A little steadier than when they'd headed out.

No more riding horses, climbing hay bales or spending time alone away from the house with Clint.

Thank goodness this job was nearing the end. She honestly wasn't sure how much longer she could resist him.

"I can't believe this place is in Medina." Clint scanned the lobby of Collins Family Rodeo. It looked like something that should be in Austin.

"Larae used to work in marketing at the rodeo in Fort Worth. She's put her heart and soul into this. It's dedicated to the memory of her mom, Laura Collins, who was killed by a drunk driver. That's why there's no alcohol served. She wanted it to have a family atmosphere and assure everyone made it home safely afterward."

"Lexie Parker, why didn't you tell me you were coming tonight?" In the concession stand, Lexie's mom propped her hands on her hips.

"Hey, Mama, I thought I'd surprise you."

Lexie's mom exited the stand and rushed over to hug her daughter. She was still tall and slender, with salt-and-pepper hair in a trendy face-framing style. He detected a hint of Hispanic in her features, so like Lexie's.

"Good to see you, Mrs. Parker." He offered his hand.

"You too, Clint." Her gaze narrowed as she shook his hand. "How many times do I have to tell you it's Stella?"

"Hey, Aunt Lexie." A little girl waved from the concession stand window. "Y'all want anything to eat?"

"It's on the house." A man tipped his hat at them from the booth.

"This is my friend Larae's husband, Rance, and their little girl, Jayda." Lexie introduced them to Clint.

"He knows, silly." Jayda giggled. "Clint goes to our church."

But Clint didn't know. Neither of them looked familiar.

"Good to see you," Rance said with a smile. "What can we get for you?"

Clint scanned the menu. "A cheeseburger with mayo,

pickle, lettuce and a sweet tea sounds good. But I insist on paying."

"We'll see. What about you, Lexie?"

"I'll have the same. But I won't come here again if you don't let me pay."

They liked their hamburgers the same way and refused freebies. Maybe they had other things in common, too.

"Fair enough. Larae will be tickled you're here, so I reckon I better take your money."

"I better get to cooking." Stella hurried back inside the concession stand.

Clint managed to dig his wallet out quicker than Lexie. Jayda took his money, then minutes later, Rance handed out two tickets, a bag and a drink holder.

"I'll get it." Lexie reached for both.

But he grabbed the bag. "I can manage this at least."

"Okay."

A guy at the turnstile tore their tickets in half, handed back the stub and let Lexie through, then opened a wide gate for Clint so his walker would fit.

A concrete barrier wall surrounded the arena with chairs lining the railing along the edge and stands climbing all four walls. The announcer's booth was at the end with the gate and pens, with box seats up high around the perimeter and sponsor signs circling the building.

"I never imagined something like this could be in Medina," Clint said.

"Larae and Rance worked really hard on it and I think it's doing really well."

"So how long have they been married?"

"It'll be a year this summer," she replied. Then quickly added, "Yes, Jayda is theirs. It's a long story."

"I didn't know your mom worked the concession stand."

"She's been the cook here at Larae's ranch my whole life and she used to work the concession stand at the rodeo in

Bandera while Daddy announced there when I was growing up." Lexie waved to the booth.

A familiar gray-haired man waved back. Lexie's Dad.

"So when Larae started this rodeo, Mama did the cooking and Daddy did the announcing to help out. But she loves to cook and he loves to announce, so they kept doing it. There is another cook and announcer now, so Mama and Daddy only work one night each weekend now."

Turning toward her, he mused, "You have an interesting family." Clint closed his eyes and listened to the crowd chatter, the bulls ramming their pens. He smelled the dirt from the arena floor, the leather of chaps and saddles. The rodeo always made him feel closer to Dad. Maybe that was why he'd kept coming back. And he still could, as a spectator.

"You okay?" Lexie frowned at him.

"Fine. I grew up traveling the circuit. Being at the rodeo is like home to me."

She bit her lip, the light dimming from her eyes.

"Why didn't you tell me you were coming?" Her dad approached from her right.

"I wanted to surprise you." Lexie hugged him.

"Good to see you out and stirring around." The older gentleman offered his hand.

"Nice to see you, too." Clint clasped it. "Most of my progress is thanks to your daughter."

"She's a gem all right. Eat your food. I gotta get back up there. Just wanted to give my girl a squeeze."

"See you later, Daddy." Lexie gave him another hug and he sauntered away. "Maybe I should come when they're working part of the time."

"Why don't you?" The very thing he loved, she wasn't into. He needed to put that on his list of why they shouldn't be together.

"It's never been my thing." But she fit right in with her

sparkly button-up shirt and jeans with flashy back pockets. The prettiest cowgirl in the place.

"Why, Clint Rawlins, it's so good to see you out and about." A woman with silver hair smiled from ear to ear at him.

"Thanks, Cora, it's good to see you, too."

"It's nice to see you as well, Lexie. I was worried since Clint hasn't been to church and his mom said he got hurt."

"I'm mending," he reassured her.

"Maybe we'll see you there soon."

"I'm planning on it." Clint had missed church, even with his radio preacher that he liked to listen to. He turned to Lexie as Cora went on her way. "I know her. That was Cora Wilkins. She's lived in Medina forever and works at the barbecue place in town."

"For as long as I can remember."

Patriotic music started up and a woman astride a white horse shot into the arena, wearing a spangly outfit and carrying a flag. A second spotlight illuminated a male singer standing in the middle of the arena, while the woman rounded the perimeter.

"That's Larae," Lexie told him. "She can't seem to keep a rodeo queen employed, so she ends up opening most nights."

"That's Brant McConnell. I love his music."

"Me, too. Him and Garrett Steele take turns here every weekend."

"Wow." He raised his eyebrows. "No wonder the rodeo is doing well."

They scanned the crowd for a glimpse of Carly and the kids. A man stopped in front of Clint, blocking his view. He greeted Clint as if he knew him, but Clint had no clue who he was and Lexie didn't know, either, so she couldn't help.

Movement out of the corner of his eye caught his attention. Cooper was waving from the first-level seating.

"There they are." He pointed to the other side of the arena.

They circled around and Clint settled beside Cooper while Lexie took a seat by Carly.

"You came, Uncle Clint!"

"I sure did. I guess we're all sitting where the old people do tonight, huh?" He shot his nephew a wink.

"Come sit by me, Lexie." Cooper scooted closer to Clint, making room for her between him and Carly.

"Okay." Lexie played musical chairs to satisfy his nephew.

Once she was by Cooper, the child promptly climbed into Clint's lap.

"You're too big to sit in your uncle's lap." Carly leaned around Lexie, giving Cooper *the look*.

"But I miss Uncle Clint," Cooper whined.

"He's not too big. I'm fine." And Clint knew Cooper meant he missed the old version of Uncle Clint. The one who remembered everything, like Cooper being seven now. His gaze went misty.

"Scoot closer to Lexie, Uncle Clint, I want to sit by her, too."

He obliged his nephew, since he wanted to sit by her, too.

Charlee squirmed in Carly's lap, reaching for Lexie. "I sit on Lexie."

"I don't mind at all," Lexie murmured, patting her lap.

"You sure?"

"I love kids."

Carly let go and Charlee scrambled over into Lexie's lap.

And he caught a glimpse of a possible future. With Lexie. And two kids. Or more…

"The Star-Spangled Banner" started up and they stood until her dad said an opening prayer.

For the rest of the evening, people passed by, told him how glad they were to see him. He knew none of them. Lexie or Carly covered and explained who each person was once they left.

"Apparently, I met a lot of new people in the last two years. And you know everyone even though you didn't live here."

"I've made lots of holiday visits and each time went to church with my parents. Most of the people you've seen tonight are from church."

"I guess our church has gotten lots of new members in the last two years," he remarked.

"It seems like it has grown during that time."

The music changed to a booming rock instrumental as the first bull rider blasted into the arena, careening atop a cream-colored Brahman. He made the buzzer and leaped to safety while the bull went after the bullfighter.

Lexie grabbed his arm and he looked over at her. Her eyes were squeezed almost completely closed. Once the bull lurched through the gate and the chute boss shut it behind him, she took a breath, relaxed.

"You okay?"

"Sorry." She let go of him, clasping her hands in her lap. "You know how I told you I'm afraid of cows? I'm terrified of bulls."

"But you grew up at the rodeo."

"And saw lots of bull wrecks. This event always makes me nervous."

Clint nodded in understanding. "I guess it makes sense to be afraid of bulls if you're afraid of cows. Feel free to hold on to me whenever you need to."

She gave him a shaky smile that made him want to shield her from anything life threw at her. But he currently couldn't shield a gnat from a fly. Lexie did not need him. She needed a real man to take care of her.

This next week would be their last week of therapy. Then she'd be gone from his life. Best to not get too attached. But that was a lot easier said than done.

Chapter Thirteen

It was a wonder Lexie hadn't dreamed about bulls last night. Yet here she was again at the Saturday night rodeo.

Coming seemed to energize Clint and part of her job was helping patients get back to their normal lives. For Clint, normal included the rodeo. Tonight they'd seen a few more people—long-term acquaintances—he knew, but getting out of the house and interacting with others seemed to help his outlook.

Still, if this kept up, she needed to get someone in his family to accompany him. Anyone other than her. Carly and the kids couldn't come tonight, so it was just her and Clint with no one to sit between them.

They found seats, then stood when the opening ceremony began. Once the prayer was over, they settled in their stationary chairs.

"Clint, is that you?" A pretty blonde hurried toward them.

"Katie?" Clint's jaw dropped.

Who's Katie? The woman was tiny, maybe five-two. If Lexie were standing, she'd feel like the Jolly Green Giant next to her.

"Are you all right? I heard you got hurt." Katie never took her eyes off him, as she gestured to the walker.

"I'm fine." He stood and the blonde looked even tinier.

"I'm so glad. I was really worried." Her arms went around his waist as she pressed her cheek into his chest.

Something in Lexie's stomach burned. She could *so* not be jealous.

Clint wrapped his arms around the blonde, engulfing her small shoulders.

"Why the walker if you're fine?"

"I had some balance issues at first. But I'm better now. At this point, it's just a precaution when I go out."

Katie blew out a big breath, obviously relieved, then pulled away from him. Her pale green eyes landed on Lexie.

"This is Lexie, my—girlfriend."

Huh?

Katie forced a pouty smile. "It's nice to meet you. I hope you're taking good care of him."

"I am," Lexie managed.

"Well, if Clint was still mine, he wouldn't need a walker, because he'd have me to lean on."

"Trust me, I lean on Lexie plenty." He settled beside her, draping his arm around her shoulders.

Her heartbeat went into overtime. If blondie ever left, she'd kill Clint for this.

"Well, I better get back to my seat. Zander will be riding soon." She did a flirty finger wave, then sashayed away.

"Remove your arm before I put you in a headlock," Lexie growled between clenched teeth.

"I can't. I'm so sorry about that."

She glared up at him. "If you're sorry, why can't you move your arm?" His ruse pulled every nerve taut since she wouldn't mind being his girlfriend, but she didn't want him using her to make blondie jealous.

"Because she'll be watching us."

"Well you should have thought of that before you lied

about me being your girlfriend." She could almost feel the steam coming out of her ears.

"We dated for six months. Before Dad got sick. Once we got his diagnosis and knew his time was limited, I moved back home to help Mom take care of him and the ranch. Katie dumped me and moved on to my ex-best friend, Zander."

"Ouch."

"Yeah. But I'm glad I found out her true colors before things had time to get serious." He winced, a contrite expression on his face. "I shouldn't have lied about who you are. Chalk it up to pride. I want her and Zander to know I don't need either of them. And admitting to Katie that I have a therapist babysitter would have made me feel really weak. Not to mention hopeless."

This illness was hard on him. Like his father, he'd always been self-sufficient and strong.

"Okay." She leaned into him. "I'll play along. Just for tonight. But we can't sit here like this all night. Number one, it's uncomfortable. Number two, she was probably watching before we ever saw her. If we lay it on too thick, she'll figure us out."

"Good point." He moved his arm. "How about we hold hands?"

"That works."

He threaded his fingers through hers, settling their clasped hands comfortably between them. "Can you look over at me adoringly every once in a while?"

"No." The problem was, she could. And mean it.

At the close of the church service the next day, Lexie and her parents filed out of their pew. Followed by Larae, her husband and daughter, their mutual friend Stacia, along with her dad and twin niece and nephew.

All the children in her friends' lives made her feel like

she was missing out. She'd been so focused on her career and whittling down her student loans for so long, and now it seemed like most people her age had kids.

Clint had insisted on coming, but his family sat on the other side of the church, and were a few pews back, so at least she hadn't had to avoid looking at him all morning. But now, there he was, vying for her attention.

"So you and your patient looked pretty cozy at the rodeo last night," Larae whispered.

"It's not what you think." She explained about Katie.

"Well it looked natural and very real. Y'all would make a great couple. And when I came in this morning, he couldn't take his eyes off you."

"I'm sure he was just looking at the stage, waiting for the service to start."

"If you say so, but what do you think he's looking at right now?"

As if of its own volition, her gaze strayed his way. Caught his.

She waved. He waved back. Then she quickly looked away.

"Well, aren't y'all just the perfect couple," Stacia murmured.

"We're not."

"Whatever you say."

"What are you girls whispering about?" Mama raised an eyebrow.

"Lexie and Clint are dating," Stacia announced, jabbing her in the shoulder. "But she's playing coy."

"We are not." Lexie's face heated. "He's my patient."

"Well, if you're not dating, what were you doing all cuddled up with him at the rodeo last night?" Larae asked, crossing her arms with an inquisitive gleam in her eye.

"We weren't. He had his arm around me for two minutes. But only because—"

"And then you two held hands for the rest of the time," Stacia said.

"You were there?"

"Dad and I took the twins last night. We were sitting right across the arena from you. One minute, I looked over there and Clint was hugging some woman. The next time I looked he was all about you."

Who else had been there? There was no telling who all had that vantage point last night. What had she been thinking?

"That was his ex-girlfriend. She did a number on him." Lexie gave a play-by-play of how she'd agreed to be part of Clint's deception. "I don't know why I went along with it."

"Well, you helped him out," Mama said, with a wink. "But once his therapy is over, I certainly wouldn't mind you dating him."

"You, too?" Lexie groaned, closing her eyes.

"He's a good Christian man. Hard to come by in this day and age."

"He's. My. Patient. I don't know what I was thinking. If anyone in the medical profession, who knows me, happened to be there last night, they might deem me unethical. I could lose my job."

"Calm down, sweetheart." Mama pushed Lexie's hair back over her shoulder. "Even if your new boss was there, he wouldn't know that Clint is your patient. You're currently a free agent."

"They'd know. His walker was sitting right there for everybody to see."

"Not necessarily," Stacia said, biting the inside of her lip. "He could be your boyfriend who just had surgery."

"Ugh. I can never show my face at your rodeo again, Larae. Or maybe even at church. Or anywhere."

"You're being a bit dramatic, I think." Her best friend

chuckled. "And besides, don't look now, but your patient is staring again."

Lexie chanced a glance at Clint and he headed in her direction. As her mom and friends promptly abandoned her.

"So this is my last week of therapy." He pocketed his hands. "It doesn't seem like it's been three weeks already."

"And Thursday's the big day when Joel gets home." She edged toward the lobby, hoping to escape him soon. Sunday was supposed to be her day off from resisting him. "I need to see if Carly and your mom need help getting ready for his welcome-home party."

"I don't think there'll be much prep. We're having a bonfire, roasting hot dogs and s'mores. Apparently, that was his request."

"The kids will love it. Who doesn't love a bonfire?"

"You're coming, right?"

"Oh, no." She shook her head. "I'll cut out once we finish your therapy that day. I wouldn't want to intrude."

"You won't be. Carly's told Joel all about you and Mom thinks you're part of the family. She'll be disappointed if you don't stay."

She smiled at him. "I guess if you put it like that, I'll come."

"Once this week is over, we'll still see each other here at church. I hope you'll stay in touch with Mom."

"Of course." She'd be at the wedding for certain. Just one more week of working with him. Then get through the wedding. And move on.

Absolutely no pining over the cowboy.

Late on Monday afternoon, the doctor scanned, poked and prodded until Clint felt like a science project. At least Dr. Arnett came to the Bandera clinic once a week, only fifteen minutes from Medina, allowing Clint to get almost a full day of therapy in before his appointment.

"Your physical improvement is remarkable."

Pride radiated through him. "I have a great therapist."

"That you do. We miss Lexie at the hospital."

After this week, he'd miss her more.

"What about your memories?"

"A few insignificant details. One significant."

"Good. Good." The doctor stared at the computer screen. "Once we get your tests back, depending on what I see, I'll determine whether to release you to normal activities. In the meantime, no driving still. I trust you have a driver once Lexie starts her new job here next week."

"My soon-to-be stepdad. He's in the waiting room."

"That's good."

"Do you think my memory will ever fully return?" he asked.

"I honestly don't know. But if it doesn't, get out there and make new memories." Dr. Arnett shook his hand. "You'll hear from me in a few days."

"Thanks, Doc." Clint stood, walking out of the exam room on his own. With no bobbles or staggers. Something he couldn't have done three weeks ago. So with the bulk of his physical abilities reclaimed, why was he still so miserable?

He'd been kind of disappointed today, when Lexie had agreed to let Ted drive him to his appointment. Who was he kidding? "Kind of" didn't begin to describe it.

After this week, he'd miss Lexie's encouragement, understanding ear and quiet strength. If his results came back okay, maybe he'd tell her that. Maybe he'd have a chance with her.

But it was a big if. The bulk of his memory was still blank concerning anything that had happened between his two bull wrecks. As long as he couldn't remember those past two years, he'd be unconvinced he could make a full recovery.

"All good?" Ted stood when he saw him.

"All good. But I still can't drive. He wants to see my test results first."

"When's that?"

"A few days."

They made their way to the elevator.

"I'll be your chauffeur." Ted took off his cowboy hat and did a little bow.

Clint chuckled. One of the richest men in Texas just bowed to him.

They made it on the elevator, to the first floor and outside. He felt odd without his walker, though he was doing fine. Just slow.

Once in Ted's truck, Clint went over the tests and scans. "I guess he'll compare them to what he ran right after my injury to see if there's improvement."

"You're gonna be fine. I can tell you're sharp as a tack. Just like before."

He blew out a breath. "I hope so."

"Your mama said you're looking for a place to rent."

"I haven't found anything yet. But don't worry, I'll move in with Carly if I have to."

"You don't have to go anywhere," Ted told him. "The ranch is your home. You've single-handedly kept it alive and turned it around into a profitable business."

"You and Mom shouldn't start your marriage with a tenant. I'll find something."

"I need you to talk your mama into moving to my place until we build a house, so you can stay at the ranch. There's no reason in you trying to find something to rent, when the ranch by all rights should be yours."

"You're renting your place right now. Right?"

Ted nodded.

"Well, what if you and Mom live at the ranch and I rent your place?"

"That could work. Then once we build a house, I'll deed the ranch to you and pay Carly like we talked about."

"We'll see. I'd rather buy the ranch."

"Stubborn like your mama. There's no way I'm taking a penny from you for something that's not mine." Ted turned toward home. "We'll see all right."

It was nice to know Mom would be okay. That Ted would take care of her. That he had Clint's back. And Carly's.

If only he could have Lexie.

Lord, thank You for helping me get better. Let the tests come back good. Let my memory return. Help me to move forward and not feel like I'm in limbo.

"Your results will be fine." Lexie pinned him with a knowing gaze as he shifted on the balance ball the next afternoon. "I can tell you're nervous. Less focused."

"I'm fine."

"Mmm-hmm."

A knock sounded at the door.

"Come in," Clint called.

Audrey opened the door, her face white.

"Mom, what's wrong?" Clint stood and walked over to her, managing to stay steady despite his hurried steps.

"Carly was on a FaceTime call with Joel, getting his flight itinerary and ETA. The screen went blank." Her chin trembled and she clasped a hand over her mouth.

He hugged her. "That doesn't mean anything's wrong. Maybe just technical difficulties."

"I pray so. But we're talking Afghanistan. Carly's certain he's under enemy fire. She's a mess."

"When will she know something?"

"Whenever whatever happened gets resolved. It could be an hour, or tomorrow, or days."

Lexie pushed down the wave of unease rising in her

throat and checked her watch. "It's almost time for school to be out."

"Carly's in no shape to pick up the kids. Or just be a mom."

"Don't worry." Lexie slung her purse over her shoulder. "I'll go get them. Charlee's at the day care, right?"

"That would be wonderful." Audrey sighed. "Maybe take them somewhere for an hour."

"Or all night, if I need to. I'll just say we're having an adventure."

"Your folks won't mind?" Clint's mom asked.

"Not at all. I'm supposed to have supper at Larae's ranch with her and Stacia. They both have kids, so I'll take Cooper and Charlee there. Is it okay if they ride a pony? She's really gentle and good with kids. I rode her when I was a kid."

"They'd love that." Audrey pushed away from Clint and hugged her. "Thank you so much. We'll go to Carly's and keep her company."

"It's not a problem. If I need to keep them overnight, I'll get them where they need to go tomorrow." She gave Audrey a good squeeze. "I better go, though. You'll call and let the school and the day care know I'm picking them up."

"I'm on it." Clint dug his phone out of his pocket. "Then I'll call Ted."

Did he want Ted around at a time like this? Or he knew Audrey needed him. Maybe both. Either way, it was a good sign.

"Take my car." Audrey handed her the keys. "The kids will recognize it and I have Charlee's car seat all ready in the back."

Lexie cut through the kitchen and out the front door.

Five minutes later, she was in the pickup line at the elementary school. Cars inched along in front of her, picking up kids. When she reached a teacher standing on the sidewalk, she rolled her window down and leaned across the passenger's side to see her.

"I'm Lexie Parker, a family friend of the Morgans. Here for Cooper."

"ID, please."

She fished her driver's license out of her purse, handed it over.

The teacher scrutinized the picture and Lexie, then handed the license back. "Sorry, we can't be too careful these days. His uncle called about you."

"I'm glad you're careful."

"I'll go get him." The teacher smiled. "Be right back."

As the cars continued inching forward, teachers escorted each child or children to the cars, making sure none of the kids got in harm's way. Small towns. It was where she wanted to raise kids. If she ever had any.

She caught sight of Cooper led by the teacher she'd spoken with. Once she came to a complete stop, the teacher opened the passenger door and helped Cooper in.

"Is something wrong?" Cooper asked.

"Nope." She caught the teacher's gaze. How much had Clint told her? "You know my friend Larae from church. She invited us to her ranch."

"Can we go in the rodeo arena?" He buckled up.

"Sure. But there won't be another rodeo until the weekend."

"I know, but it'll be cool to check things out anyway."

With Cooper successfully sidetracked and chattering about the rodeo, she inched along and finally exited the pickup line. A few miles down the road, she repeated the process at the only daycare center in Medina. The teacher there checked her ID as well, then brought Charlee out.

"Aunt Wexie," Charlee said with glee as the teacher handed her over.

She'd never called her that before. "Hey, sweetie. How was your day?" Reminded her of when Jayda was little.

"Super."

"I'm so glad." Lexie buckled the toddler in her car seat. "How would you like to ride a pony?"

"Yay!" Charlee clapped her hands.

"I'm too old to ride a pony," Cooper huffed.

"Well, maybe you can ride a regular horse, then."

The teacher waved. "See you tomorrow, Charlee. Cooper, you have fun riding."

"Thank you," Lexie said, as the teacher shut the door for her.

"Where's my mom?" Cooper obviously knew something was up. "Why aren't you helping Uncle Clint walk?"

"We finished therapy early, so everybody could get busy at the ranch getting ready for your dad to come home. So I thought we'd have some fun."

"I could have helped." Cooper pouted.

"I know. But Charlee's too little to help and I wasn't sure she'd want to go ride without her big brother. Okay?"

"I guess."

She wouldn't be able to sidetrack Cooper for long. He was old enough to know something wasn't right. *Lord, please keep Joel and his unit safe. Give Carly good news. Soon. Let all of the soldiers come home to their families as planned.*

Chapter Fourteen

Lexie sat on the porch at Larae's ranch, sipping lemonade with her two best friends while Cooper rode a horse and Charlee, Jayda and the twins rode ponies, supervised by Lexie's dad.

"Cooper knows something is up. I don't know how long I can distract him."

"You're doing fine." Larae patted her hand.

"Thanks for the behind-the-scenes arena tour. He loved it."

"Anytime."

"I don't know if I could be a military wife," Stacia admitted, pushing off with her foot to set the porch swing swaying again.

"Me, neither." Lexie closed her eyes. "I can't imagine how Carly must be feeling."

"You're pretty attached to this family. Especially when it comes to Clint." Larae shot her a knowing smile.

"No, I'm not, at least where he's concerned. I'm just trying to help them out."

"You've always been a great at that," Larae reminded her before turning toward Stacia. "Back when my dad had his first stroke and moved in with us in Dallas, Lexie was awesome. Lola, my landlord at the time, was a great babysitter for Jayda, but she and her husband were older. On the weekends, Aunt Lexie would swoop in and whisk Jayda away to Six Flags or the zoo."

"Like some rock star aunt. I always dreamed of having one of those." Stacia laughed. "Ready for the new job?"

"Past ready," Lexie admitted.

"You don't realize it now." Larae wagged a finger at her. "But you'll miss Clint."

"Will not."

"Mmm-hmm. You're still going to the wedding, right?"

"Of course. I think the world of Audrey."

"What are y'all wearing?" Stacia sipped her lemonade.

"Rance bought me a new pale blue dress. It's really pretty."

"To match your eyes." Stacia set her glass down and began fiddling with the chain links of the swing. "I'm wearing aqua. I get so tired of green just because of my hair, but it's hard to find colors that don't make me look pale or weird."

"Your hair is gorgeous with all those honey and red highlights," Lexie told Stacia, then turned to watch the kids round the barnyard again with Daddy grinning from ear to ear. "Women pay a fortune to fake your natural color."

"So what are you wearing, Lexie?" Larae pressed.

"I haven't really thought about it."

"Go with that red one you've never worn." Stacia's tone held a note of longing. "I love red, always wanted to wear it, but it clashes with my hair. You're gorgeous in red."

"Thanks." Lexie traced the condensation on her glass with her finger. "But it's so flashy. I don't know why I bought that dress. I'm thinking navy."

"That's it, I'm coming over before the wedding." Larae pointed at her. "You're wearing the red if I have to tie you up and dress you myself."

"Have you found an apartment yet?" Stacia changed

the subject, in an obvious effort to soothe tensions, the way she always did. Larae and Lexie had been friends to begin with, then Stacia and Larae. As they'd become a threesome, Stacia had fallen into the role of peacemaker.

"I haven't looked. Mama and Daddy seem so offended every time I mention it."

"Clint will love you in red." Larae wouldn't let it rest.

Lexie rolled her eyes.

"Just admit you've got a thing for him," her best friend prodded. "And besides, in a few days, he won't be your patient anymore."

"His brain isn't a hundred percent and I don't have a thing for him."

"You should definitely wear the red." Stacia winked. "Reel him in."

"You, too? I can't believe you're ganging up on me."

"Sorry." Stacia winced. "But I saw the thing in your eyes, too. You like this guy and we just want you to be happy."

"I'll make you a deal. If you'll get a love life, I will, too."

Stacia laughed. "We're both doomed, then. With the twins, the store and the ranch, I don't have time to think. Much less get a love life." Her tone filled with longing again. "But sometimes I do get lonely. I mean it's crazy, I've got the twins and Dad, but sometimes I wonder what it would be like to have a good Christian man in my life."

Lexie could be much more specific. She wondered what it would be like to have *Clint* in her life.

Gravel crunched and a white car came into view.

"Who's that?" Larae shaded her eyes with her hand.

"Carly." Lexie stood. "If it was bad news, she wouldn't be driving. Right? Clint would have called to prepare me. Told me what to do with the kids…"

"Looks like she's smiling, waving at the kids."

Lexie blew out a deep breath. "Thank You, Lord."

Carly parked the car. With a wave to Lexie, she headed for the barn. The passenger-side door opened, and Clint stepped out, then strolled in her direction.

"Yep. He's got eyes only for you." Larae waved at him. "See, he didn't even notice me."

Stacia grinned. "At least we got your mind sidetracked with all the talk of him."

"Everything okay?" Lexie asked as soon as he was near enough to hear.

"She got an email from his unit. The internet server was down. All the soldiers are safe and due to be home Thursday, as planned."

"What a relief!" Lexie pressed a hand to her heart.

"Yes. Carly's been an emotional wreck. We can't thank you enough for sparing the kids all that."

"I enjoyed them, but I'm glad everything's okay and that y'all came. Cooper was suspicious. I didn't tell them anything, just kept them distracted."

"Ladies." He greeted Larae and Stacia, as an afterthought, then looked toward the barn. Carly was headed to the car with both children. "Looks like we're leaving. See you tomorrow, Lexie."

"Bright and early."

He waved, strolled away.

"And he likes you." Larae elbowed her.

Stacia chuckled. "A lot."

"Y'all are *impossible*."

Impossible, unless he fully recovered with his memory intact, and no permanent brain damage.

Otherwise, she could only get through the next few days, then the wedding, and hope not to run into him again. While they lived within five minutes of each other and attended the same church.

But no matter how often they saw each other, as long as

Clint's brain was scrambled with his emotions and choices in question, her heart couldn't go near him.

The door of the therapy room blasted open and Cooper burst into the room. "Uncle Clint, let's go fishing!"

"Cooper, I told you to wait until Clint's finished with therapy." Carly stopped in the hall, pointed her son toward the door. "Out. Now."

"It's okay, we were just finishing up for the day," Clint told her, pulling the key from the treadmill. He was glad to be done anyway. Though he'd mastered the treadmill, it still took a lot out of him.

"I try to teach him restraint and you give him whatever he wants." Carly's gaze narrowed.

"That's what uncles are for."

"Can we, Uncle Clint? Can we?"

"I don't know, ask my boss." He motioned to Lexie.

"If it's okay with your mom, I think fishing is just what the doctor ordered."

"Yay!" Cooper did a fist pump in the air.

"Do I have to take my walker? We'll ride down to the river in the Mule."

"Not a mule like a horse," Cooper clarified. "It's a cross between a four-wheeler and a golf cart."

"On steroids," Clint added, as he managed to step off the treadmill.

"My dad uses one at the ranch where he works and I'd say that's a pretty accurate description. Hmm." She tapped her chin with a forefinger, looking way too cute. "If you ride the Mule and take it slow once you get there, the walker can skip the trip."

"Yay!" Clint mimicked his nephew.

"Can you come too, Lexie?" Cooper asked.

"Um." She grimaced. "I'm not sure. I don't like worms. Or fish. Uncooked, anyway. The fish, not the worms. I wouldn't even like worms if you cooked them." She did a little shudder.

"I'll bait your hook and if you catch anything, I'll get the fish off for you." He clasped his hands together as if in prayer. "I promise, you won't have to touch anything slimy. Pleeeeeaaaaase come!"

Clint was torn. With wanting her to go. And wanting to escape her.

She chuckled. "How can I turn down an offer like that?"

"Yay! I like your scrubs." Cooper's face scrunched up. "But it's not Independence Day."

"Precisely," she said, gesturing to her navy scrubs sprinkled with heart-shaped flags. "I'm patriotic all the time."

"Cool. I'll go get my tackle box." Cooper darted from the room.

"See if Charlee wants to go, too," Lexie called after him. "That is if it's okay with you. I'll let the guys fish and keep her away from the water."

"Fine by me." Carly started to close the door. "Sorry. Finish up and I'll distract him."

"It's okay, we really were finished." She checked her watch. "Fishing will be good therapy. Fine motor skills, reasoning and hand-eye coordination."

"Please." Clint shook his head. "Don't turn fishing into therapy. It's about fun. And food."

"Therapy can be fun." She shot Carly a wink. "Like jigsaw puzzles."

"Not that again," Clint growled. "I'm outta here."

"I'll go change, but I have no idea where I'm going, so somebody better wait for me."

"Don't worry, I'll wait." Clint's gaze caught hers. He'd wait until she wasn't his therapist. Until his memory came back. If it did, she'd be fair game.

"Be right back." She scurried out of the room.

As if she couldn't wait to escape him. So even if he remembered everything and the doctor gave him a clean bill of health, that didn't mean she was interested. He longed for and dreaded next week. Lexie would be gone from his daily life. A blessing. And torture.

By the time she'd gone to her car, grabbed her clothes and changed, Cooper had his tackle box and Clint had gathered up several fishing poles.

Why had she agreed to go? At the end of their therapy session, she'd been home free for the evening, with only three days left to work with Clint. Three days left to resist him.

Could she get out of it? Nope. Not without disappointing Cooper.

"Here you go." Clint held a pole toward her.

Charlee clasped her hand and squealed, "Charlee go fishing!"

"Sorry, guys, I'm out." She scooped up the adorable toddler. "I'm on Charlee patrol. We're gonna pick flowers and watch."

"Oooh. Flowers."

She rubbed noses with Charlee and got giggles in return. "Every girl needs wildflowers."

"Okay, let's pile in the Mule." Clint opened the garage door, ushering them through.

"I've never ridden in a Mule." A two-seater. "How will we all fit?"

"I'll ride in the bed," Cooper volunteered. "I won't stand up and Charlee can sit in your lap while Uncle Clint drives."

"Uncle Squint drive."

"But your doctor said no driving."

"I don't think this counts. He meant on the highway, with other traffic."

"Drive slow," Carly cautioned.

"I always do when the kiddos are with me." He climbed in, patting the seat beside him.

Cooper clambered into the bed, sat down and held on to the roll bar. "Come on, Lexie. Let's go."

"Why don't y'all come, too?" Lexie hoped there wasn't pleading in her tone. "I can walk if you want to ride, Audrey."

"Actually, that's a good idea." Audrey linked arms with Carly. "After the turmoil we had going on yesterday, we could all use some fun. But only for an hour or so. That way we can get back in plenty of time to clean up and go to Wednesday night Bible study."

"What happened yesterday?" Cooper eyed each of the adults.

"Just some stuff with your father." Carly covered. "The internet server was down and I couldn't get in touch with him to find out when his flight lands. But it's all worked out now."

"He'll be here, tomorrow. Right?"

"Of course. In fact, he's already on his way." Carly squeezed Mom's hand. "I need to change clothes, so we'll walk. It's not that far. Go ahead, Lexie."

"I'll take Monkey until you get in." Clint reached for her, sat Charlee in his lap between him and the steering wheel, while she crawled in. Lexie tried to leave space between her leg and his as she retrieved Charlee.

"Drive, Uncle Squint."

"Yes, ma'am." He started the engine, then slowly drove away. "Everyone wave bye to your mom and Grandma. And by the time they get there, we'll have caught supper. Slowpokes." Clint drove off.

Once they got out of the yard, she saw that Mule tracks had cut a permanent path through the woods over the years. Live oaks lined the way with a smattering of wildflowers. Mexican hats with their drooping gold and red petals had always been her favorite, but they didn't usually show up until May. Then she heard the river before she could see it. The soothing flow of water over a rock bed.

The trees parted, revealing a swath of shallow spots, deep and seemingly bottomless in others about ten feet wide. Cypress trees lined both sides with fat, clawlike roots reaching hungrily into the water.

Clint killed the engine and he and Cooper unloaded all the gear while Lexie tucked Charlee against her and climbed out of the vehicle. With the toddler settled on her hip, she strolled over to the water.

"Charlee wanna swim."

"It's too cold for that, Monkey." Clint tucked his arms against his chest and did a fake shiver. "Brrr. Cold."

"Brrr. Cold." Charlee mimicked him.

It was a tie on which one was cuter at it.

"Your uncle Clint is right. We have to stay out of the water. And never, ever, ever come to the river without an adult."

"Never, ever, ever." Charlee shook her head, then peered into the water in deep concentration.

Lexie followed her gaze and spotted a school of minnows. "You see all those tiny fish, don't you?" Rocks led across the river and she carefully used them as stepping stones, then sat on the largest one near the minnows and planted Charlee in her lap.

The little girl leaned forward and peered into the water. "Here fishy, fishy."

"She's heard our neighbor call her cat." Cooper giggled. "I don't think fish come when you call them, Charlee."

"Most cats don't, either," Clint added wryly.

Cooper sat his pole down, then hopped the rock trail out to where they were. "Those would make great bait. I wish we had a trap. Remember that trap you made last summer, Uncle Clint? We need to make another and leave it here overnight."

"You'll have to remind me how to build it." Which meant Clint didn't remember. The familiar dullness settled in his eyes the way it did every time he couldn't summon a memory.

"Mommy! Grandma!" Cooper hollered. "You made it. Come see the minnows."

The two women followed the stepping stones out to see.

"They're pretty," Audrey said. "Shimmery."

"They're called golden shiners." The boy pointed at the pool. "That one's big. Come see, Uncle Clint."

"I'm not sure Uncle Clint's balance is quite that good yet." Carly tried to deter him. "I'm sure he's seen a minnow that big before anyway."

"I can do it." Steely determination set his jaw.

And Lexie knew they wouldn't be able to stop him.

"Let me help you." She handed Charlee to Carly. Then Audrey stepped farther across, so Lexie could get by.

She followed the rock trail back to the shore to where an impatient Clint had already taken a few steps.

"I don't need help."

"Humor me." She offered him her arm.

He latched on, obviously aware he was pushing his capabilities.

Slowly, they made it a few rocks at a time. Until Clint wobbled. She turned to try to steady him. But it was too late.

Everything went into slow motion. Him going down. Taking her with him. Cold soaked her backside, then her entire back, stealing her breath as she squealed. Clint's muscled arm was around her middle as he landed on his side beside her with a splash that soaked every part of them both.

"Brrr. Cold," Charlee said.

"You okay?" Lexie's teeth chattered through the question.

"Fine." He pushed up onto his knees and offered her a hand. "You?"

"Freezing."

"I could have done it if you hadn't tried to help," he muttered, his pride obviously injured.

"Probably. But I didn't want you to fall."

"I appreciate the thought." He slicked his water-soaked hair back from his face.

"Y'all will catch your death," Audrey called. "Get out of there and back to the house."

"But I wanna fish," Cooper whined.

"Y'all stay." Clint stood, then managed to help Lexie up. "I'll take her back to the house, get dried off and warm, then come back with the Mule to pick up the kids and the gear."

"I'll bait the hooks and take care of any fish we catch," Cooper volunteered.

"We'll probably just watch you." Audrey waved a hand at Clint. "Will y'all please get out of the water."

"I don't think we need to worry about trying to stay on the rocks anymore." She turned toward the house side of the river.

"No. But our feet won't be as wet if we do." Clint climbed up on a rock, raising his arms out to his sides like a tightrope walker.

She followed with her arms out, so he wouldn't be embarrassed.

He made it to the shore, then turned to face her. "See. I just needed my arms."

"Me, too, apparently." She made a few bobbles on purpose to make him feel better.

"There's a blanket under the seat of the Mule," Audrey hollered. "Wrap up in it, until you get back to the house."

"Yes, ma'am." Clint saluted her, ushered a shivering Lexie to the Mule, then dug under the seat for the blanket.

With them both seated, he wrapped the blanket around their shoulders, started the engine and turned toward the house.

"I'm really sorry, Clint. If I'd let you do it, you probably would have been fine."

"It's not your fault. I shouldn't have tried it." He frowned. "Thanks for acting like you needed your arms to balance and those few fake wobbles you threw in to save my pride."

"You're welcome. Pride goeth before a fall."

He chuckled, then burst into a full-out laugh, as she joined in.

They made it to end of the path, into the yard. He pulled up right by the front sidewalk, killed the engine and turned to her.

With fingers shaking from cold, he pushed a damp tendril away from her face. "I'm gonna miss you, Lexie Parker."

His words put a hitch in her heart as his gaze lowered to her lips.

"I think I better go home to get warm." She turned away, flailed her way out of the Mule. Somehow, on trembling legs, she made it to her car, started the engine, turned the heat to full blast and backed out of the drive.

She'd miss him, too.

After all the warnings she'd given herself about falling for him, not a one of them had worked.

Chapter Fifteen

While Ted gathered wood, Clint tried to be useful. He'd managed to hang a Welcome Home banner between two trees, and string twinkle lights in the branches behind the firepit. Without getting on a ladder. And mostly avoiding Lexie.

Cooper and Charlee ran amok, overenergized, waiting for Carly to return from the airport with Joel in tow. Which was exactly why she hadn't taken them with her. Mom was busy preparing food, while Lexie made frequent trips back and forth, bringing out paper plates, cups and plastic cutlery.

At some point, she'd changed from her sea life scrubs into jeans paired with a sequined purple tee and her blue jean jacket.

Even though last night she'd proven in no uncertain terms that she wasn't interested him, he couldn't seem to ignore her.

After two final days of therapy, she'd be gone from his life. He'd continue overseeing his ranch and being careful not to overdo it until his doctor released him to normal activities. She'd move on to her new job. But he couldn't imagine not seeing her every day.

"They're here!" Mom called from the back porch.

Cooper and Charlee ran around the house to the front yard, while Ted and Clint headed for the house to cut through.

He glanced back at Lexie. "You coming?"

"I'll let y'all welcome him and meet him later."

"You're welcome to join us," Ted encouraged.

"I know. I'm fine out here. Y'all go on."

Clint was torn about seeing Joel. He was thrilled to have his brother-in-law back. They'd become close over the years. But he still felt weak and incapable and didn't want Joel to see him like this.

By the time he made it into the kitchen, Joel strolled in with Cooper in one arm and Charlee in the other. Both kids clinging, their faces buried in their father's shoulder.

"Well, aren't you a sight for sore eyes." Joel raised an eyebrow. "You really don't remember anything that happened from the last two years?"

"Not a thing."

"Including that hundred bucks I owe you?"

"I think it's coming back to me." Clint grinned. "Now that you mention it."

"Maybe this is my chance to finally beat you in arm wrestling again."

Clint guffawed. "So you're saying it takes me with a brain injury for you to win?"

"Whatever it takes." He hugged Clint around the kids. "Missed you, bro."

"You, too." Clint's throat clogged, eyes burned.

"Thanks for being here for these knuckleheads."

But had Clint been there? He had for two years, but he couldn't remember. And then he'd risked his life riding a bull. What would have happened to Cooper and Charlee if he'd died? If Joel hadn't come back from Afghanistan? Would Ted have been a father figure for them? Probably, but it was Clint's place.

No more risks. Carly and the kids would need him whole and healthy if Joel got deployed again.

Mom and Carly entered the kitchen.

"Okay, Ted," Mom announced. "Now that our guest of honor is here, you may start the bonfire."

"I'm on it." Ted clapped Joel on the back. "Glad you're home, son."

Mom and Carly busied themselves, getting hot dogs, buns, condiments and s'mores ingredients ready to carry outside.

"Arm wrestle, Uncle Squint."

At the moment, Charlee knew him better than she knew her daddy.

"We could have a quick round," Joel agreed, sitting down at the table.

"Bring it." Clint settled across from him, completely unsure of his arm wrestling abilities.

"You two." Carly rolled her eyes.

The kitchen door opened and Lexie stepped inside. "Ted needs lighter fluid."

"I'll get it." Carly rifled through the cabinet. "Joel, this is Lexie. Lexie, this is my Neanderthal husband."

"It's a tradition." Joel propped his elbow on the table, flexed his hand and winked at Charlee. "When me and your mommy started dating, your uncle Clint wanted to arm wrestle me. I soundly beat him."

"Your daddy had been in the air force for two years, including boot camp, where all they did was build muscle. And I was only sixteen. But after a few years, he couldn't beat me."

"But Uncle Clint couldn't beat me, either."

"So who won?" Lexie asked.

Carly snickered. "They spend hours straining their muscles, but no one wins."

"And your daddy wants to take advantage of your poor

old brain-damaged uncle now, thinking he might win." Clint pouted for effect.

"It is pretty sad when you put it that way," Carly remarked as she handed Lexie the lighter fluid.

And Clint wished his pretty therapist would go back outside. Not watch him get beat. But she lingered.

He put his elbow on the table, flexed his hand, sent his brain a message to make his hand fight.

"Ready." Joel gripped his hand. "Set. Go."

Clint closed his eyes, pushed against Joel's hand. Managed to hold steady.

"I call a time limit of two minutes." Mom chuckled. "Or we'll never get to eat. Here, Lexie, you keep time and I'll take this to Ted." She retrieved the lighter fluid, then stepped out the back door.

Hands at a standstill. But Clint was starting to tire. Thank goodness for Mom's time limit.

An eternity passed, but Clint managed to hold his ground.

"Time!" Lexie announced.

Joel's hand relaxed. He grinned as he let go. "Well, you may have lost some marbles, but not any muscle. I guess I'll never beat you, bro."

"Okay, children." Carly grabbed a sack of hot dogs. "And I'm including the two overgrown ones at the table. Let's take this party outside. Everybody grab a bag to carry out."

Joel flashed a smile. "It's nice to officially meet you, Lexie."

"You, too."

The women and kids filed out, carrying bags, while Joel and Clint nabbed what was left.

"So Carly failed to mention Lexie is a looker. And she had eyes only for you, just now."

"Trust me. She only sees me as a patient, probably afraid I'd strain myself."

Joel winked. "I think it was more than that."

"Well, it can't be."

"Why?"

"Because I can't remember anything from the last two years."

"I know that must be weird, but what does that have to do with Lexie?"

Clint sighed heavily. "I was here when Dad got sick. The first thing to go was his memory."

"That doesn't mean you'll end up the same way," Joel reminded him. "Carly said it was a brain injury. Your dad had several concussions on top of concussions."

"Who knows if it was the first one or the fifth one that did him in. I can't pursue a relationship with that hanging over my head."

His brother-in-law narrowed his eyes at him. "But you can't keep your life on hold."

"I can. And I will."

"For how long?"

"Until I know for certain I'm okay." He hurried as best he could toward the door, longing for the day when he could say his piece and make a dramatic, quick entrance.

He finally made it outside.

"Uncle Clint, watch." Cooper walked the heavy benches surrounding the firepit like he was on a balance beam.

"That's awesome, bud."

"Can you do this?"

At the moment, he probably couldn't. "Not as good as you, I bet."

At least he didn't have to use his walker anymore. Even outside. He'd just have to hold on to the progress he'd made physically and pray his mind bounced back, too.

And forget Lexie. She was perfect. Good with kids, she

understood him and his need to run his ranch. And she was beautiful. If only his brain didn't have a kink in it that might derail his future.

Two more days and she'd be out of his life. Something he looked forward to. And dreaded.

"I've never had a s'more with a Reese's before." Lexie moaned. "So good."

Cooper giggled over her reaction, tugging a smile from Clint.

"Why did I never think to make them this way? The chocolate bars never melt good the other way." She really wasn't exaggerating. It really was *that* good. Hot, bubbly marshmallows, toasty graham crackers, oozing melted chocolate and peanut butter.

"You've officially lived now, Lexie." Carly chuckled. "Glad we could help you out."

Thick, chunky beams lined the firepit, forming a hexagon shape. Lexie had one length to herself, with Clint to her right. Ted and Audrey sat on one side, leaving space between them probably for Clint's comfort. Carly and Joel cuddled, all armed up as Lexie's grandmother used to put it, with Cooper and Charlee in their laps. They'd obviously missed each other. Seeing the reunited family put a pang in Lexie's heart. Would she ever have a special someone?

Her gaze collided with Clint's and her cheeks promptly heated.

"Can I have another, Mommy?" Cooper asked, but he was already sliding two marshmallows onto his skewer.

"Just one more, but then I'm afraid we'll have to take the guest of honor home because it's your bedtime."

"Aw, Mommy," Cooper whined.

"I'm kind of tired, too." Joel yawned. "And I'm looking forward to officially being home, sleeping in my own bed."

"Okay." Cooper hovered his marshmallow over the fire. "I put an extra one on for you, Lexie."

"Thank you. I'll take you up on that." She readied the crackers and Reese's Cups.

The marshmallows turned golden and Cooper stuck them toward her.

"Careful," Carly cautioned. "You don't want to burn Lexie."

Lexie placed the Reese's-laden crackers on each side of the marshmallow and pulled it off the skewer, then handed it to Cooper and repeated the process for her own.

"I like to mash mine together real good." Cooper squeezed his crackers tight. "But you have to let it cool longer before you can eat it."

Lexie followed his example. Marshmallow, chocolate and peanut butter oozed out the sides.

"I want 'nother," Charlee said.

"I'll fix it for you." Clint grabbed a skewer, then slid two marshmallows on. "I might need another, too."

Even if he didn't remember Charlee's birth and part of Cooper's life, he was a great uncle. And even though he'd recovered most of his physical abilities, she still felt like a failure. Despite the cognitive exercises, memory games and photo albums, a very large hole remained in Clint's memory.

"You can eat yours now, Lexie," Cooper instructed, then took a huge bite of his.

She sank her teeth into the goo. "Mmm…"

"You're funny, Lexie." The boy giggled. "Most adults don't make noises when they eat or roll their eyes back in their head."

Not a pretty picture he painted of her. "I can't help it. So good." She took another bite. "Mmm…"

Clint finished making his and Charlee's s'mores. "Here you go, kiddo. Be sure and let it cool."

"It's nippy out tonight." Audrey warmed her hands in front of the fire. "I'm certainly glad Clint and Lexie didn't catch pneumonia after their little dip in the river yesterday."

"You should have seen them." Cooper jumped up and told the story for Ted and Joel, then proceeded to act it out. "Uncle Clint was like this." He careened to the right, opened his eyes and mouth wide. "And Lexie was like this." He careened to the left, made the same face, but twisted his mouth to the left. "You should have seen the splash they made."

Everyone laughed at his antics, including Lexie and Clint.

"Thanks for the play-by-play, son," Joel said, chuckling. "I almost felt like I was there."

"I don't think that was the face I made." Clint groaned. "It was more like this." He crossed his eyes, stuck his tongue out to one side.

"All I know is the water was cold." Lexie shivered.

"Brrr. Cold." Charlee hugged herself.

Their laughter mingled.

"This is so fun, but I'm afraid we need to head back to the house." Carly stood. "I hate to leave a mess, but I really need to get this guy home."

"I'll clean up," Lexie offered.

"I better git, too." Ted got up. "I've got an early board meeting in the morning."

"Everybody put their trash in the bag." Audrey started gathering debris.

"You go see Ted off," Clint told his mom. "I'll help Lexie and put the fire out."

The kids made their rounds of hugging, including Lexie, making her teary. Then everyone drifted to the house, leaving her alone with Clint.

"Want another s'more?"

"You read my mind." She shivered. At the chill? Or Clint?

"You cold?"

"A little."

He stood, poked the fire up, then took off his jacket and put it around her shoulders on top of hers.

"Thanks. But I don't want you to get cold."

"I won't." He settled beside her, loaded two marshmallows onto a skewer and held it over the fire.

His nearness set all her nerve endings on alert.

"So two more days of therapy."

"And we're done." She lined four graham crackers on a paper plate, set a Reese's Cup on two of them. "But you're doing great. Keep doing the exercises and the games and you'll continue to improve."

"All set for the new job?"

"I still need to find an apartment. But there's no rush. Mama and Daddy would love for me to live with them permanently."

"Why don't you?" he asked curiously.

"I don't know. It's different for you, Clint. You stay here to help your mom out. But I feel like a third wheel living with my folks. I guess I need to feel independent."

He stilled, gazing off in the distance. Their marshmallows caught fire.

"Clint, you're charring them."

He jerked the skewer out of the fire, blew the flame out. "Sorry. I'll make you another."

"It's okay, I actually prefer blackened." She sandwiched a marshmallow and pulled it off, handed it to Clint, then repeated the process.

"Me, too. They get gooier that way."

She set her hand on his arm. "You okay? It's like you went far away there for a minute?"

"Something you said about living with your parents

and me helping Mom out struck a chord. I think I almost had a memory."

"That's great."

"Do you think it'll ever all come back for me?"

"I don't know. But I do know permanent memory loss is pretty rare." She looked over at him and said softly, "Maybe you should stop worrying about what you can't remember. I mean your family has filled in most of the blanks for you. Just move forward. Make new memories."

They ate their s'mores in silence. She managed to keep quiet about it, but she closed her eyes and savored the taste.

"Watching you makes me relive the first time I ate these."

"So good." She finished the last bite and stood. "I better get going."

"Can you help me with one more thing?"

"Sure."

"Cooper asked if I could walk the beams before everybody came out tonight. I'm the one who used to hold his hand until he found his balance. But I was afraid to try. I didn't want to fall in front of him. I'd just like to know if I can do it."

"Let's see." She offered her hand and stepped up onto the beam.

He took it, stood. A frown formed between his eyebrows as he climbed up beside her. A slight bobble, but he balanced without her help.

"Looks like you can." She turned away. "Let's walk around it."

Hands still clasped, he followed.

"You're doing great."

They completed the hexagon of beams. She stopped, pivoting to face him.

He captured her other hand. "Thank you. For all your

help. Your encouragement. For having faith in my abilities, when I didn't have any."

"You're welcome. But you've been a pretty easy patient. Think you can get down from there by yourself?"

"Yes. Thanks to you."

She watched until he was safely down. "See you tomorrow." She waved, turned away, then hurried to the house to retrieve her purse.

But inside, Ted was still there helping Audrey clean the kitchen.

"You outta here?"

"I can help Audrey. You said you needed to leave."

"You don't have to do that." Audrey clasped her hands. "I can't tell you how grateful I am for all you've done for my boy."

"It helps when the patient is determined to recover. He reminds me a lot of Levi."

"Me, too." She turned to Ted. "Did you pay her?"

"Duh." Ted shook his head. "I'm not sure I'll be around anymore this week, so I wanted to go ahead and get square with you."

"I'm not worried about it. You can mail it to my folks."

"It won't take a minute," Ted said, pulling his checkbook out of his back pocket.

The back door opened. "The fire is officially out." Clint stepped inside, saw Lexie. "I thought you'd be gone by now."

"I stopped to help your mom clean up."

"I can help her. You can take off. You, too, Ted."

"Since I do have an early day, I'm gonna have to take you up on that." Ted kissed Mom's cheek. "I'll walk you out, Lexie."

She led the way. "See y'all tomorrow."

Outside, Ted pressed a check into her hand. "The best money I ever spent."

"I still feel like it's too much. And I haven't completed the job yet. I still have two days left."

"It's not too much and I know you won't cut and run. I hope to see you now and then. You'll be at the wedding?"

She smiled brightly. "Definitely. Let me know if the date changes."

"We will."

Lexie made it to her car and he opened the door for her.

"Thanks for helping Audrey's boy… I don't know what we'd have done without you." He shut the door, waved and turned toward his truck.

Just two more days and the torture of spending her days with Clint would be over. Except that she already missed him.

Chapter Sixteen

As Clint made it back from the mailbox, Lexie pulled into the drive. He stopped, waiting on the steps for her.

Her car door opened. "Look at you waiting on me for a change."

"I can't help it if you're a slowpoke," he teased.

"Someone's cocky this morning." The tropical palm trees and smiley-face suns decorating her scrubs matched her perkiness.

He opened the door for her, then set the mail in the stack on the desk in the foyer. But the pile toppled. Envelopes fluttered to the floor in all directions.

"Oops." Clint knelt to pick it up.

"Here, let me help you," Lexie said, scurrying over.

"I've got it." His hands stilled as he stood. "What's this?"

"What?" Mom strolled over beside him.

"An RSVP. For your wedding. Two weeks away?" Clint's heart stuttered. "Why didn't you tell me the wedding is so soon?"

"We've been thinking about postponing since your accident," Mom admitted, stooping to gather the rest of the mail.

"Jim and Darla Smith are coming." He held out the

RSVP. "Not only do I not know who they are, but I didn't know the wedding date had even been set."

Mom sank into her chair at the table. "I should have done it already, but I kept hoping—I want you to remember how much time has passed, to remember Ted. I can't get married with your brain stuck two years ago. With your father's passing so fresh for you."

A knot clogged his throat. He swallowed hard. "I don't want you to postpone. No putting your life on hold, just because mine is."

"The wedding can wait."

"No, it can't. I'm fine with it." He ambled toward the foyer, faster than he used to be at least.

"Where are you going?" Mom called.

"I have to get something out of my truck." He hurried for his truck, as quick as he could and still remain upright, then opened the door and looked back toward the house.

Mom stood on the porch, a deep furrow between her brows.

"Stop worrying. I'm fine." He waved her inside.

Thankfully, she went, shutting the door behind her.

He found the magnetic key holder under the rear fender, climbed in the truck, fumbled to extract the key and started the engine.

The doctor hadn't cleared him to drive yet. But he'd made significant progress since he'd last seen Dr. Arnett. He had to get away. To think, clear his head. He'd just have to focus and be careful.

Checking behind him twice, he backed up, pulled down the driveway and turned toward town.

But where? Where could he go? Carly was busy with the kids and Joel had just gotten home. Apparently, he didn't have any friends. No one had come to see him since his accident. For the last two years, he'd obviously kept to himself, focused on the ranch.

The only person he could think of that he wanted to talk to about all of it was Lexie. But she was back at the house.

Clint knew he really didn't need her as a therapist anymore. He could feed himself, walk without his walker, button his own clothes. Yet, she was such a good listener. But since she obviously wasn't interested in him, it was better for his heart if he cut her loose now.

The church loomed in the distance. Maybe someone neutral would be the perfect ear for his troubles. And the preacher had been there two years ago, so Clint actually remembered him.

"Do you think he's okay to drive, Lexie?" Audrey asked, wringing her hands in her lap.

She hoped so. "He's made a lot of progress. He's capable. And Dr. Arnett will probably release him once his test results come back." Lexie sat at the breakfast bar with a defeated Audrey. "Does he have any friends he might go to see when he's upset?"

"None that live here anymore. He pretty much kept to himself for the last few years, concentrated on the ranch." Audrey straightened the salt and pepper shaker, then resumed wringing her hands.

Ted captured one of her hands. "He and Joel are close, but Clint wouldn't want to interrupt his first day home with Carly and the kids."

"I shouldn't have called you away from your board meeting," Audrey said. "You should go back."

"It's fine. We rescheduled for later in the day." Ted tucked her into his shoulder. "Clint's always been friendly with the ranch hands, but most of them haven't been here over two years."

Audrey leaned into her fiancé. "Even the ones that have, he never did anything with them outside of ranch work. I doubt he knows where any of them live, and I don't think he'd confide in any of them."

"What about from the rodeo?"

"They're still traveling the circuit and I'm pretty sure he lost touch with them. I don't think he was ever close with any of them except Zander. And their friendship hit a wall a few years ago."

A wall named Katie.

"Anywhere he liked to go, just to think?" Ted asked. "Somewhere that gave him peace?"

"Not that I can think of." Audrey closed her eyes. "I just wish I knew where he is. That he's safe."

Ted wrapped his arms around her.

"Oh, wait, the church! He's always loved our church. And Pastor Douglas has been there for five years, so Clint would remember him." Audrey pulled away from Ted and grabbed her purse. "We have to go."

"I'll drive," Ted offered, following her to the garage door.

"Wait." Audrey stopped. "He's upset because of us. Our wedding." She turned to Lexie. "Would you go?"

The last thing she needed was to be comforting Clint. He was way too good-looking and emotionally damaged, and her heart was bound to get broken by this man. But how could she turn down his mom's plea for help?

"Sure." She shouldered her purse and headed for the foyer. "I'll let you know when I find him." She hurried out to her car, started the engine, then pulled onto the highway.

It was well within her wheelhouse to calm patients down. She'd taken a few counseling courses in order to be a well-rounded therapist and been complimented by patients, doctors and nurses on her soothing presence. But she'd never had to calm down a patient she'd fallen for. This could get sticky.

She'd have to keep a professional distance. No hugging or comforting. Just talking and reasoning.

The church was only a few miles from the ranch. As it came into view, she saw his truck, blessedly in one piece.

Once she parked, she sent his mom a text that he was at the church.

She stepped inside the lobby, looked down the hall toward the office. Probably talking to the preacher. But first, she scanned the sanctuary.

A dark-haired man hunched on the first pew on the right. It was him, looking much like he had when she'd first started working with him, defeated.

She strolled toward him. When she was a few pews behind him still, he raised his head and looked her way.

Had he been praying? "Hey," she whispered. "Sorry to interrupt, but your mom's worried."

"I'm fine."

"That's good. Because you're not supposed to be driving."

"I was careful and it's not far. Dr. Arnett will probably release me this week."

"Probably." She settled beside him on the pew, with a good two feet between them. "But he hasn't yet. From a medical standpoint, you're basically driving illegally."

"They can't postpone the wedding."

"Your mom just wants you to be at peace."

"I am. Mostly." He blew out a rough breath. "Except that it seems like my dad died just yesterday. But it's been two and a half years. And now there's Ted. I genuinely like him, I really do. It's just—"

"Hard realizing life went on without you for two years."

"Yes. I should have asked about the wedding." He tipped his head back and looked toward the ceiling. "I sensed they had a day set, but deep down, I didn't really want to know."

She threaded her fingers through his, trying to concentrate on comfort and comfort only.

He squeezed her hand. "Shouldn't I be remembering by now if I'm going to?"

"All patients are different, all injuries are different. Some recover quickly, some take longer."

"But I'm not. I'll end up just like my dad. It'll all go downhill from here."

"You don't know that. And there's no reason to assume it. Your dad's illness didn't come from one bull wreck. There were a series of concussions involved."

A muscle ticked in his jaw. "But you can't tell me if it was the second one or the sixth one that caused his decline."

"No. Not for certain."

"I appreciate you working with me this last month. I really do. But I'm recovered physically enough, and there's no reason to drag this out any further. You're free to go."

Her heart sank. "But we still have two days left."

"I'll never forget everything you've done to help me, Lexie. But I don't need you any longer." He pulled his hand away.

"Okay." Even though she wasn't ready to let him go yet. "I guess we're done then."

The door of the church opened and Lexie turned to see who was there. The morning sun flooded over them and she couldn't see through the glare.

"Oh, Clint, I was so worried." Audrey hurried down the aisle.

As the door closed, Lexie saw Ted hesitating in the back.

"Thank you for finding him." Audrey smiled. "I need to talk to my son."

"Sure." She stood and rushed toward the door, blinking away moisture.

Ted held it open for her, then followed her out.

"How is he?"

"Upset." She willed her tears away. "But it's more about not being able to get his memory back than the wedding. He's recovered enough physically and since he knows all the exercises, he'll continue to improve. But he's convinced his memory isn't coming back."

"But there's still hope, right?"

"Of course." She swallowed hard. "But he doesn't want me to come anymore."

"I'll talk to him."

"No. He's right." She felt a tremor coming on, took a deep breath. "He can do the exercises, play the games without me. He'll continue to get well, whether I'm there or not." She dug in her wallet for the check. "I haven't cashed your check. I can't accept the full amount, since I shorted you two days."

"Which is not your decision. You signed on for the salary I quoted and that's what I intend to pay you. Keep the check. I know you're starting a new job, but is there any way you could work with him a few hours a week? Maybe on the weekend?"

"I'd only be wasting your money." And her heart couldn't take any more of Clint.

"Clint's health isn't a waste to me."

"He really doesn't need me anymore." The check still seemed like too much, but she was officially debt free. If only her heart hadn't gotten involved. "But I still don't feel right about taking the full amount."

"I do. That boy couldn't even feed himself when he first got out of the hospital. Within days, he could do that and brush his teeth. Your therapist skills are priceless."

"Please feel free to call me if y'all need any help or advice."

"I will." Ted gave her a hug. "Thanks for everything, Lexie."

"It was my pleasure." But as she walked to her car, with enough money to pay off her student loans in her hand, she couldn't help but feel like a failure. She hadn't been able to help Clint recover his memory. And even worse, she'd fallen for him.

On autopilot, she climbed in her car, started it and pulled away. Leaving Clint behind.

"You okay?" Mom settled beside him on the pew.

"You can't postpone the wedding."

"I can't go through with it when you don't even know Ted."

"But I've gotten to know him. And I really like him, Mom. Dad would like him, too."

She clutched his hand, swiping at her tears. "I'm glad you think so. But sweetheart, your health is the most important thing to me."

"Your wedding has no effect on my health. I won't let you put things on hold because of me. I won't." He flashed a crooked grin at her. "Besides, how on earth could you alert everyone who's been invited that they're uninvited when you've only two weeks to do it? We have family members who are flying in, right?"

"Aunt Jenny and Uncle Felix are coming from Wyoming."

"I want your wedding to be only good memories, Mom. Not chaos and rescheduling. This thing is going off without a hitch. As scheduled. Period."

"Are you sure?" She slid her arm through his elbow, leaning her head on his shoulder.

"I'm positive. Do I have a tux?"

"You're supposed to have a final fitting this week."

"Then let the wedding preparations begin!"

"But no more driving for you until Dr. Arnett releases you."

"I promise." He sighed. "I think I remember why I wanted to buy the ranch in Fort Worth."

"Really? Why?"

"I found a distributor interested in selling our meat, but I'd need more stock to keep them supplied. I decided to move there because I didn't want Ted to feel like a third wheel. I wanted you to begin a life with him. The two of you. Not with me in your guest room."

"Oh, Clint." Her chin trembled. "That's so sweet. So you remembered that?"

"A while back, Lexie said something about getting her own place because she feels like a third wheel at her folks' place. And then Ted mentioned needing a distributor so we can go bigger with sales than our online business. It hit a chord and I remembered."

"I'm so glad." She tapped his temple. "Maybe it will all come back now."

"I hope so."

"Ted and I were afraid you wanted to move because we made you feel like a third wheel."

"Not at all."

"Well, if the ranch in Fort Worth is still available, it all sounds great to me. Except for the you-moving-there part. Ted wouldn't mind at all for you stay at the ranch permanently and it wouldn't make him feel like a third wheel, either."

"Newlyweds need space. They don't need adult stepsons hanging about."

"Not true. But if you're determined to find your own place, I hope you won't move all the way to Fort Worth." Mom closed her eyes. "You could find a place to rent nearby. And besides, you'll have to oversee things here at the ranch. Ted is a lot of things, but a cattleman, he's not.

So you might as well stay close. Unless you really want to move. I only want you to be happy."

"If it's okay with you, I'd like to stay near Medina." He covered her hand with his and squeezed it. "But I will see if the Fort Worth ranch is still for sale and get my own place."

"You'll always be my baby boy and I'd love to keep you close. But don't do anything permanent or sign a long lease. Ted wants to build a house for us. A house where his wife never lived and where your father never lived. A house for us to begin fresh. He wants to deed the ranch over to you."

Clint nodded. "He mentioned it during one of our walks. But I can buy it."

"Nonsense! You will *not* buy your inheritance."

"We'll see. What's your holdup on the new house?"

She shook her head and blew out a breath. "Marrying money is so complicated. I just don't want anyone to think I married for money. That I'm a gold digger. If we live at the ranch, that'll prove it."

"You can't worry about what other people think, Mom. As long as Ted knows you love him and not his money, that's really all that matters."

"How'd you get so smart?" She patted his cheek.

"I guess the part of my brain the bull didn't step on is still firing."

"I've been so worried about you."

"Don't be." He kissed the top of her head. "I'm on the mend."

But was he? Would his memory keep coming back? Or was this one tidbit all there was?

"I officially let Lexie go," he admitted.

"Why?"

"She'd done as much as she could with me." And his heart couldn't take her constant presence a minute longer.

But he missed her already. "At this point, what will two more days accomplish?" Besides, hopefully Dr. Arnett would call with the results today. If the news was bad, he wouldn't be up for therapy.

"Whatever you think, then. But you need to keep doing the things she showed you, so you can keep getting better."

"Don't worry. I will."

He should have known it could never work out between them. If she was all flustered about merely pretending to be his girlfriend, she certainly wouldn't be interested in a real relationship with him. Best if he kept his distance from her. Something he'd been telling himself since day one. And it obviously hadn't worked.

His phone rang, and he dug it out of his pocket. Didn't recognize the number on the screen, but it was from San Antonio. Maybe Dr. Arnett's office. His hand shook.

"Hello?"

"Is this Clint Rawlins?" The woman's tone was professional.

"Yes."

"I'm calling from Dr. Arnett's office. He'd like you to come in this afternoon, to our San Antonio office if possible. But if you can't make the trip, you can consult with Dr. Finch at our Bandera clinic."

"San Antonio is fine." His heart skipped a beat. It could only be bad news. If it was good, a nurse would tell him over the phone. He'd rather talk to his doctor than someone he didn't know. "What time?"

"Can you make it at two o'clock?"

"Yes. I'll be there. Thank you."

"Was that the doctor?" Mom asked as he slipped the phone back in his pocket.

"Dr. Arnett wants to see me today at two."

Mom clasped her hand to her heart. "I'm sure everything's fine. He probably just wants to go over your results in detail with you."

"That's probably it." He stood. "Let's go home."

This afternoon, he'd learn his prognosis. Would he follow in Dad's footsteps?

Chapter Seventeen

As soon as Ted put the truck in Park, Clint got out and hurried toward the clinic.

"Slow down there, we're not in a race," Ted cautioned.

But Clint was in a race for his life. Today he'd learn if he should plan his future. Or if his brain was done for. With only decline and forgetting more and more each new day to look forward to. Until his lungs forgot to breathe and his heart forgot to beat. Like Dad.

Inside, he rushed to the window, forced himself to make pleasantries with the receptionist and signed in.

"It's gonna be good news. I just know it." Ted's positivity grated on Clint's nerves.

"Do they call you in for good news?"

"You have to keep your hopes up."

Not if there was nothing to hope for. "I appreciate you bringing me." It would have been hard on Mom or Carly. He'd have felt weak with his mom or sister chauffeuring him around.

"No problem. You got this."

Mom and Carly had both wanted to come, but Ted had assured them he'd call as soon as they spoke with the doctor. He wasn't sure he was up to putting on a strong front for them. Truth be told, he was a wreck inside. Downright terrified, he'd prayed the entire drive there.

"Mr. Rawlins?" a nurse called.

He couldn't seem to get up, just stared at her.

Ted gripped his arm, urged him to his feet and ushered him toward the nurse.

She led them into an exam room. "Dr. Arnett will be right with you." Then she left them alone, shutting the door behind her.

"Want a magazine?"

"I don't think I remember how to read at the moment."

"Just look at the pictures." Ted shuffled through a stack and held up a copy of *Texas Monthly*. "There's an article on page twenty-three about beefalo."

Clint couldn't manage to take it from him.

"I can't wait until April 8," Ted chattered. "The day I marry your mama, I'll be the happiest man on earth. Did I tell you we're taking a road trip in the motor home to the Grand Canyon. She's so all-fired determined not to take some lavish trip, worried everyone will think she only wanted my money. Neither of us have ever been to the Canyon, so I figure it's high—"

The door opened. Dr. Arnett stepped inside, offering his hand. "Morning, Clint. I asked you to come in today because I want you to see the results of your scan."

The doctor sat down in front of a laptop and punched several keys. An image popped up.

"This is your original scan." Dr. Arnett pointed to a dark area. "Here's your frontal lobe. This dark area shows where the injury took place. The dark means function has been damaged." He punched some more keys. "Let's take a look at your new scan."

Clint held his breath as Ted gripped his shoulder.

The scan came up. Was it just him, or was there less dark?

"The second scan shows less damage. Less dark. Your

brain is repairing itself." The doctor showed him another result that measured his brain waves. The results in the second test showed improvement, as well. "I wanted you to see the results for yourself, so you'll believe what I have to tell you."

He started breathing again. "What does it mean?"

"It means I foresee a full recovery for you. There's no sign of permanent damage or brain atrophy. I'm releasing you to normal activities. But there is one thing I have to refrain you from and I'm afraid you won't like it." Dr. Arnett's tone was grim.

"What's that?"

"Given your history, and your dad's, I can't release you to return to the rodeo."

Clint laughed. "That's okay. I don't want to go back."

"Perfect."

"What about my memory?" he asked.

"I still think it will come back. Just give it time." Dr. Arnett shook his hand. "I won't need to see you again. Unless you have any problems, which I don't foresee. But keep me updated as your memory returns."

"Thank you, Doctor." Ted clapped him on the back. "Let's get out of here, my boy." He tossed Clint the keys. "You can drive my truck."

Giddiness settled in his soul. *Thank You, Lord.* "Let's see about that tux Mom mentioned. I've got a wedding to go to in a few weeks."

"Me, too. I hear she's the prettiest bride in all of Texas."

"Agreed." The only one Clint could imagine being prettier than Mom, was Lexie.

Normal. His brain was returning to normal. He could drive. Do anything he wanted. Other than rodeo, which was officially off his bucket list anyway. In fact there was only one thing he wanted. *One person.* Lexie.

If his memory ever fully returned and he felt whole, there'd be nothing holding him back from going after her.

The manager pointed out all the amenities the apartment had. It was cute, homey. No yard to have to maintain. Community washers and dryers included with a pool, and exercise equipment.

But it was in Bandera. "I'll take it." Maybe living in Bandera would be better. There'd be less chance of running into Clint.

"Great. I'll just need first and last month's rent, plus the deposit we talked about."

"Here you go." Lexie handed over the check.

"You wrote it already?"

"I'm desperate. As long as there aren't any pests, I'll take it."

"I assure you, we have an exterminator spray all of our units quarterly." She detached a key from a huge ring and handed it to Lexie. "Welcome to Yellow Rose."

"Thank you."

The manager left.

Fully furnished. All she had to do was get her clothes and a few sentimental items from her parents' house.

She strolled to the window. It was peaceful here. When it got a bit warmer, she'd enjoy the pool.

Maybe if she got her things settled in her new place, she'd feel less scattered. Lexie exited, made sure the door was locked, then darted for her car, just as a man came out of the office. She smacked right into him. Hard chest.

"Oomph." The air went out of her lungs.

He caught her upper arms. "Are you all right?" Clint's voice.

It couldn't be. Just her imagination. She kept staring at the third button on his shirt. Hunter green. The color Clint often wore. It made his eyes look even more intense.

"Lexie, are you okay?"

"Fine." She forced her gaze up to his. "Just stunned. What are you doing here?" She took a step back.

His hands fell to his sides. "If you had run into me like that a month ago, I'd have gone down. And taken you with me."

"So you're renting an apartment here?"

"After the wedding, I planned to move into the house Ted is renting. But his landlord has another interested party, so I just wanted to see what's available. Unfortunately, nothing here. The last one bedroom lower level just got taken." He shifted his weight to the other leg.

Something he couldn't have done a month ago, either. "That would be me. I actually wanted the upper level just to get natural exercise from climbing stairs, but there weren't any one bedrooms available up there."

"And there's nothing in Medina. I checked."

"Me, too." She sighed. "Medina is so small there aren't a lot of rental properties to be had."

"Living and working in Bandera will cut down your commute."

"It's only fifteen minutes from Medina," she reminded him.

"I know. But I'm sure you'll appreciate the lack of commute at the end of a long day. Do they allow pets here?"

"No." Her shoulders sagged at the admission. "I'll just have to keep my ears open for something else. But this will do for now."

"How was your first day at work?"

"Good." She'd enjoyed working with her patients. But it had seemed as if she was only going through the motions. Preoccupied. Missing a certain cowboy.

How had she let this happen? Gotten hung up on her patient. Thank goodness he hadn't been able to get an apartment here. She had to stop thinking about him. Stop running into him. Leave him in the past.

"I remembered why I wanted the ranch in Fort Worth." He explained the memory he'd captured.

And she tried to listen. But he was just so distracting. "That's really great that you remembered, Clint. A very good sign."

"It hadn't sold yet, so I'm buying it after all. But we'll still see each other around. Missed you at church yesterday."

"I had a lot to do." She felt guilty about skipping Sunday services. Maybe she needed to find another church. Somewhere Clint didn't attend. At least until he moved.

"Maybe I'll see you at the rodeo sometime."

Not if he was in Fort Worth. "I really don't hang out at the rodeo." She grimaced. "And I can never be seen there with you again or ever pretend to be your girlfriend again."

"Okay. But that's not what I meant."

"Apparently lots of people saw us holding hands last weekend. If anyone in the medical field got wind of it, it could make me seem unethical. And possibly even hurt my career."

His lips twitched. "Even though I'm officially not your patient anymore."

"I just don't need any rumors at my new job."

"Understandable. Well, I better get going. We're having Charlee's birthday party tonight if you want to come."

"I hate to miss it."

"But you have a lot to do?" he guessed.

She nodded. "Are you driving?"

"Yes. I saw Dr. Arnett Friday. He released me to drive and resume normal activities. But Ted's with me to supervise and appease Mom's worries." He turned away. "By the way, the wedding is in less than two weeks, as originally scheduled, in case you still plan to come."

"I do." She had to. *Wanted* to. If she could just get through the wedding. And find a different church, hopefully here in Bandera, maybe she wouldn't have to see Clint again. And maybe she could forget him. "I'm glad you're doing well." Unable to stop herself, she gave him a quick hug that cracked her heart in two, then forced herself to let go and take a step back.

"Bye, Lexie." He waved before strolling toward his truck. An easy gait he hadn't had a month ago. A quiet confidence she hadn't seen before. Made him even more attractive.

Ted waved from the passenger's side. She returned his greeting with a smile.

Maybe she'd come down with the flu. That way she'd have to the miss the wedding. Even though she wanted to witness the beginning of Audrey's well-deserved happily-ever-after, she didn't need to see Clint again. Ever.

Only thing—it wasn't flu season.

Chapter Eighteen

April 8 turned out to be the perfect, sunny spring day for a wedding.

"The dress is too much." Lexie scrutinized the other guests. She was officially the only one wearing red.

"No it's not. It's perfect." Larae followed the usher to their seats.

White chairs lined the lawn of the church. Since Audrey had married Levi here, she'd wanted something different this time. So the wedding was outside on the grounds.

"You've officially got the perfect man, Larae," Stacia said, scanning the crowd. "I can't believe Rance volunteered to keep the twins for me today. Mason can be a handful."

"I suspect he partly volunteered so he could skip the wedding." Larae laughed. "The only one he ever actually wanted to attend was ours. But he loves kids. And since we only have Jayda, he hasn't had a chance to be around a little boy much. They'll have fun."

"Are y'all planning to have any more?" Lexie asked.

"We've talked about it. But Jayda's eight. It would be a big age difference."

"They'd still bond, I'm sure." Stacia filed into a row of white chairs with Lexie in the middle. "If I ever get married, I wish I could have cousin-siblings for the twins someday."

How had they all made it to twenty-seven, with only one of them married? With Stacia raising her twin niece and nephew, she had her hands full. And Lexie had always been focused on her career. But now she was beginning to regret that. Since meeting Clint. He made her think about all things domestic.

She had to stop thinking like that.

Music started up. Traditional violin, but she couldn't put her finger on the piece. At the back of the gathering, a curtain swept aside and Charlee toddled down the plastic sheeting that formed an aisle, dropping flowers as she went, picking up some, and dropping them again as the crowd chuckled over her cuteness. Next Cooper followed, holding his satin pillow as ring bearer. Carly strolled down the aisle after him, smiling.

The music swelled into the opening strains of "Here Comes the Bride." The crowd stood as Clint escorted Audrey down the aisle.

His gaze caught hers and locked. Try as she might, she couldn't look away. Finally he got close enough to her aisle that he had to break eye contact.

Audrey's dress was champagne colored, tasteful and perfect for a second wedding. Ted waited at the altar unable to take his eyes off her. Lexie completely understood.

They reached the flowered archway.

"Who gives this woman to lawfully wed this man?"

"My sister and I." Clint placed Audrey's hand in Ted's, then moved beside the groom to serve as best man.

Lexie dabbed at her tears.

The preacher welcomed everyone, said the opening prayer, and the guests settled in their seats. As the ceremony began, Lexie tried to pay attention, but her gaze and thoughts strayed to Clint.

His eyes widened and he swayed for a moment.

Had something upset him? Lexie focused on the pastor's words. Typical vows. Was Clint still upset about his mom marrying Ted? Her attention returned to Clint.

He'd gone pale. Would he pass out in the middle of his mother's wedding?

The preacher had gone on too long. What was wrong with him? If this shindig didn't wrap up pretty soon, Clint would need to sit down. But he couldn't interrupt the ceremony. Ted would think it was on account of him. And it wasn't. Last night's rehearsal dinner had been tiring, but good. He'd re-met Ted's family and liked them. They all loved Mom.

His head hurt.

Flashes of the two years he'd lost burst through Clint's memory. Almost losing the ranch, saving it, investing in beefalo and turning a profit. Joel getting deployed not long after Dad died, spending more time with Cooper, Charlee's birth. Meeting Ted, getting to know and like him, him asking for Mom's hand. Meeting his family.

Hearing about the ranch in Fort Worth, meeting with Mr. Thomas and his banker, deciding to move and give Mom and Ted a fresh start. One after the other the puzzle connected into a trail of events ending in his last bull ride.

He remembered all of it. Just like that. In the middle of Mom's vows with Ted. He closed his eyes, trying to refocus.

"I do," Mom said.

At least he'd heard that part.

"By the power vested in me, I pronounce you husband and wife. You may kiss your bride."

Mom and Ted kissed, with lots of joyful laughter and hugging.

"Ladies and gentlemen, I give you Mr. Theodore and

Audrey Townsend. What God hath joined together, let no man put asunder."

The crowd applauded.

"The Townsends request your presence at the reception. They're going to cut the cake and greet guests and then disappear for pictures. So please, once the bridal party exits, feel free to follow."

A joyful rendition of the bridal march started up. Charlee scampered down the aisle, followed by Cooper, then Carly. His turn. Thankfully, he was feeling steady again. As he made his way down the white plastic sheeting, his gaze strayed to Lexie. Still totally rocking the red dress. Mom and Ted followed. The family lined the sidewalk to the church doors.

"Mom," Clint whispered. "I remember."

Her smile widened. "What do you remember?"

"Everything."

She closed her eyes and hugged him tight. "Oh, that's wonderful! Thank You, God. Thank You. That's my perfect wedding gift."

"And you still approve?" Worry dulled Ted's eyes.

"Definitely." He embraced the older man. "I remembered during the vows. I could have stopped it if I'd wanted. But I didn't want to."

"I'm so relieved."

"Why? We've always gotten along and developed a really great relationship. Twice."

"I know. But I was worried you wanted to move to Fort Worth because deep down, either you didn't approve or you couldn't stand to stick around and watch your mama move on."

"None of the above. I remembered my reason weeks ago and I figured Mom told you." He went over the deal with the distributor and his reason for planning to move. "I competed in the rodeo for a down payment on the ranch and decided to move to get out of your way so you and Mom could have a fresh start."

"Oh. Silly boy. I hope you know I'd rather have you close."

"I do now."

"I'm glad we're finally on the same page." Ted hugged him back, dragging Mom and Carly into the huddle.

"You make our mom very happy. And after Dad, I was afraid she'd never be happy again."

"I'll be a sight for pictures. You two are making me all sappy and I'm smearing my makeup."

"You can't be anything but beautiful." Ted beamed at her.

If a man could glow, Ted was doing it.

"What's going on?" Carly asked. "I couldn't hear all the whispering."

"I remember everything."

Carly's eyes widened. "That's wonderful."

They reformed their line, greeted guests, accepted countless congratulations. Lexie was a few people away. He figured she'd skip him or maybe even scurry away, not even hug Mom to avoid him. Now that he had his memory back, they needed to talk.

"Audrey, I'm so happy for you both." She embraced Mom, then Ted, and started to move away.

"Hey wait. What about me?"

She turned, shook his hand.

"I need to talk to you."

"I'm holding up the line."

"After pictures. Can you stick around?"

"I don't know. That could be a while. And I'm still settling in at my apartment. I was hoping to get some pictures hung tonight. Try to make it feel like home."

Clint elbowed his mom, hoping she'd help him out.

"Oh, Lexie, you have to stay for the reception. And

could you help me with my makeup before the family pictures? I'm afraid I need some repairs since I got a little soggy."

"Of course."

The line finally ended and Mom and Ted headed inside to cut the cake. The photographer went to work, capturing the moment while Clint located Lexie near the door.

"They'll be at this for a while." He strolled over to her. "How about that talk?"

"Um. Okay."

Through a sea of guests, Clint escorted her toward the lobby.

"Ms. Parker, it's nice to see you outside of work." A man wearing a suit waved at them.

"Dr. Earle, I didn't see you."

"How have your first few weeks at the clinic been?"

"Good. I really like it there."

"I'm glad." He offered his hand to Clint. "Didn't I see you with Lexie at the rodeo a while ago?"

Lexie's cheeks pinked. "This is my boyfriend, Clint Rawlins."

He forced his jaw not to drop.

"It's nice to meet you, Clint. Good to see you off the walker."

"Clint had a bull wreck a month ago, but he's all mended now."

"Must be handy to have your own personal therapist." Dr. Earle smiled. "You're Audrey's son, right?"

"Yes."

"Ted and I have been golf buddies for years. I'm glad to see him happy again. Your mom seems really great."

"She is," Clint replied. "Ted's been good for her."

"Well, since I've already congratulated the happy couple, I'll be on my way. See you Monday, Lexie."

"I'll be there."

Clint led her to the adult classroom and shut the door behind them. Hopefully, they wouldn't be disturbed.

"Oh my goodness." She cupped the top of her head with her hands and began pacing the room. "He saw us at the rodeo. Do you think he bought the boyfriend thing?"

"I do. Calm down. Even if he didn't, he can't prove anything."

"You're right." She sucked in a deep breath. "I've known your mom for a long time, we could have met years ago. We'll just have to ask Ted to play along with us."

"What happened to you not being able to pretend to be my girlfriend?"

"I panicked when he mentioned seeing us at the rodeo. If he saw us the night we were pretending for Katie, I couldn't let him think you were my patient." She closed her eyes. "Now he'll expect me to bring you to the company picnic in a few weeks."

"I might have a solution for that."

"A fake breakup?"

Or something real. "I remember the last two years."

"Really? When?" she asked.

"During the vows."

"I thought something was going on. You looked like you might pass out up there. Do you remember everything?"

"I got flashes until everything fit. Like the puzzle in my brain got unscrambled and all the pieces fell into place."

"That's wonderful." She hugged him. "I'm so happy for you."

The feel of her in his arms was heady. "I can live now."

She pulled away and stepped back. "I'm glad."

"Can I see you? I mean, after today?"

"I don't see the need." She slipped into professional mode, as if donning a jacket. "Your balance and fine motor skills are almost back to normal and now your memory is intact."

"I didn't mean on a professional basis, Lexie. I want to see you on a personal level. Maybe take you to that company picnic you mentioned." He held his breath. Did she feel the same way he did? Or was he simply a patient and that was all he'd ever be to her?

"No more pretending." A vise grip tightened around Lexie's heart. "I'll tell Dr. Earle at the picnic that we broke up. Or if I get my nerve up, I'll tell him it was a joke, that I panicked and was pretending both times he saw us."

"I don't mean pretend. I'm interested in something very real with you."

"Huh?" Her pulse raced. "I've told you, I don't date patients. And besides that, you're moving to Fort Worth."

"But I'm not your patient anymore and I'm not moving to Fort Worth. I plan on staying here in Medina."

"What about the rodeo?" She took a deep breath. "Back when Daddy announced and I worked the concession stand in Bandera, I saw my first bull wreck." She shuddered. "I decided right then and there, I'd never date a bull rider. And all the rodeo injuries I saw at the hospital in San Antonio reinforced that for me."

"Number one, I don't want to go back. I got into it because it's what Dad did. But I never loved it like he did." He shook his head, stuffing his hands into his pockets. "Once he got sick and I left the circuit, I didn't miss it. Since then, I've only been back twice. To save the ranch two years ago, then a month ago to buy the ranch in Fort Worth."

Laughter and chatter echoed down the hall. He paused until the guests passed by.

"I'm buying the Fort Worth ranch so I can supply the meat distributor I told you about. But I don't want to move and Ted doesn't want me to, either. It worked out for me to rent his place until he and Mom build a house, then I'll move back into the ranch."

"They're probably looking for you." She took a step toward the door. "For pictures."

"They'll come get us if they need us," he murmured, slipping her hand into his.

Her breath hitched at his touch. "So what's number two?"

"Dr. Arnett released me to normal activities, but due to my history and Dad's illness, he refused to sign a rodeo release for me. So even if I wanted to, which I don't, I can't go back to the rodeo. And even if he rethinks things in the future and releases me, I won't go back. Trust me, Lexie, two concussions are too many for me and I've learned my lesson. Bull riding isn't a sport to compete in sporadically."

"What do you plan to do?"

"Run my ranch. Hire a crew to run the one in Fort Worth. Raise beefalo. Stay here in Medina, eventually marry and have kids. And I don't want my kids losing me slowly and prematurely the way I lost Dad." He took a step closer to her and clasped her other hand in his. "So what do you say? Will you have dinner with me after this shindig?"

She nibbled her lip.

"What's holding you back? Are you not interested in me?"

"I'm very interested." Her cheeks warmed. "But what if you don't know what you want? The part of your brain that was injured controls emotion. What if everything's in a jumble? It may not be a good time for you to start a relationship."

"When I saw Dr. Arnett for my results two weeks ago, I didn't have my memory back. He told me to make new ones. But my scans showed improved function and no permanent damage."

"More great news!" She squeezed his hands and gazed up at him. "I've been so worried about you."

"Which means you care?"

"Yes," she admitted softly. "I've tried really hard not to. To only think of you as a patient. But it totally didn't work."

"Listen, even before I lost the last two years, the time surrounding Dad's death has always been a blur for me." His voice caught. "But the one thing I remembered during that time was seeing you at the funeral. I think we should explore why you made such a memorable impression on me." He took another step, closing the gap between them. "So how about that dinner? Even though I remember everything, I'd like to make new memories with you."

"Okay."

"Yes!" He let go of her hand long enough to do a fist pump.

She laughed.

"I've wanted to kiss you since you trimmed my beard for me."

"I've wanted you to kiss me since then, too." Her lips tipped up in a tremulous smile. "Maybe even before then."

"Do you think we could pretend we've already had dinner and it's time for a good-night kiss?"

Breath stilled, she could only nod.

"I really hope I don't miss." He let go of her hands, framed her face with his and lowered his lips to hers.

He didn't miss. Tender, gentle and electric, all at the same time.

She lifted her hand to his cheek. The scruff of his beard soft against her fingers.

The door opened and they sprang away from each other.

"Well, look what we have here." Carly smiled from the doorway.

Lexie's face warmed.

"I talked her into dating me."

"I see that. If you two can tear yourselves away, we're ready for family pictures." With a knowing smile, Carly left them alone.

"Oh no." She clasped a hand to her rapidly beating heart. "I was supposed to help your mom with her makeup."

"That was a ploy to get you to stay so we could talk. And more." He brushed his lips against hers again, caught her hand and led her toward the sanctuary.

"I'm really glad I stayed." Her heart was all aflutter.

"Me, too." He kissed her hand.

"Stop it, so I can act like we haven't been hiding in the classroom kissing."

"Oh, I'm sure my sister will fill Mom in. But don't worry, she'll be happy for us. She's loved you for longer than I have."

Her feet stalled. "We've only known each other a few months."

"Long enough, Lexie Parker. You are very easy to love."

Her heart promptly melted into a puddle.

Epilogue

It had taken a year for Ted and Audrey to build the new house. The housewarming party had been fun and cozy with family, friends and church family. Instead of bringing gifts, everyone brought a donation to the Neurological Research Institute in honor of Levi. They'd nibbled finger foods and visited into the evening.

With everyone gone and cleanup done, Lexie and Clint had been the last ones to leave.

He slowed, pulling the pickup into his drive.

"Um, I thought we were going somewhere for dessert." Lexie frowned.

"We are. Trust me."

"I love their house." She undid her seat belt. "It's a lot like this one."

"Mom didn't want to go overboard with some fancy mansion, and since she loved our ranch, Ted went with it. With a few added features she always wanted. Vaulted plank ceilings, a porch the length of the house and dormer windows." He killed the engine, got out and came around to open her door.

"It's good to see them so happy."

"It is." He helped her down from his truck, leading her around the side of the house.

"Dessert is in the barn?"

"You'll see."

They passed the tree where they'd had their long-ago picnic as well as the barn where they'd checked on his herd so many times during his therapy. Then he led her to a path in the woods where they'd driven the Mule to fish and ended up getting a dousing.

She quirked a brow. "Dessert is in the woods?"

"Sort of. Remember the picnic we had that time? Back when I was a wobbly mess and frustrated as all get-out?"

"How could I forget?" Lexie grinned up at him. "After you ordered me to leave you alone, I watched from the kitchen window while you cleaned up."

"You did?"

"I couldn't just leave you out there."

"Were you falling for me, back then?" he asked.

"I was fighting falling for you. But it wasn't working very well."

"I was falling for you, too. Literally physically falling every time I stood up." He chuckled. "But emotionally, too."

A trickle of water sounded in the distance. "The river?"

"You guessed it."

"Please don't take me fishing." The trickle turned into lapping as they got closer. "Remember, I don't touch worms or fish." She scrunched her nose. "Too slimy."

"No fishing, I promise. Close your eyes."

"You're not planning to shove me in the river again, are you?" She grinned but obeyed.

"Never." He slipped behind her, his hands came over her eyes, and the warmth of his arms and spicy scent engulfed her. "Keep walking. I won't let you fall."

The very thing she'd once said to him. A knot formed in her throat. His complete recovery still made her teary sometimes.

The lapping became babbling.

"Okay, you can open them." His hands fell away from her face.

She opened her eyes. The river was five feet away. White river rocks and cypress trees lined the edge, with water cascading over the shallow bed. The trail of boulders she remembered zigzagged across the ten-foot span, with a picnic set up on the other side.

"I thought it was time for another."

"I love it." The patchwork quilt with the wicker basket invited her over, where a stack of wood waited for a fire. "What's in the basket?"

"S'mores makings, of course."

"Yum."

He tugged off his boots and she did the same, then he caught her hand and tugged her toward the trail.

"When we first met, I didn't think I'd ever be able to do this."

"I knew you would." She squealed when her toe dipped in the water. "Brrr. Cold."

"I've got a fire ready to start." Hands clasped with him leading the way, they balanced on each rock until they got across.

"I think I bobbled more than you did." She laughed.

He did a little bow and gestured her ahead. "Your s'mores await, my lady."

"Why, thank you, kind sir." She curtsied, strolled over to the blanket and started to sit. "I love s'mores, but you didn't have to go to so much trouble."

"Wait."

She turned around.

Clint was down on one knee.

A gasp escaped her, followed by a high-pitched giggle. She clasped a hand over her mouth as her heart went into overdrive.

"My dad proposed to my mom over a picnic with a

campfire and I want us to have as happy a marriage as they did. Only longer."

"Sounds good." Her words came out a breathy whisper, as her heart hammered, and tears rimmed her lashes.

"Lexie Parker, I've loved you for a year." He opened a velvet box. A solitaire diamond sparkled. "Maybe even longer. Like from the moment I saw you when I woke up in the hospital. Will you do me the honor of marrying me?"

"Yes!" She nodded like some giddy bobblehead. "I love you too, Clint."

He let out a whoop, slid the ring on her finger, stood, then picked her up and swung her around.

"I think I've loved you from the moment I saw those green eyes in the hospital," she whispered.

"Love at first sight until the end of time."

She pressed her lips to his. "I can't believe I'm saying this, but I'm sort of glad that bull stepped on your head."

"I'm not sure how to take that."

"If it hadn't, you'd have moved to Fort Worth and we might never have officially met."

"You've got a point." He kissed her.

Until she forgot all about bulls, rivers, rings and s'mores. Just him. Her fully mended cowboy making her heart whole with kisses sweeter than s'mores.

* * * * *

Look for the next book in
The Hill Country Cowboys series
by Shannon Taylor Vannatter,
available January 2021 wherever
Harlequin Love Inspired books
and ebooks are sold.

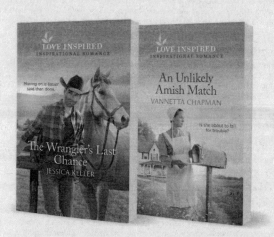

COMING NEXT MONTH FROM

Love Inspired

Available July 21, 2020

HER AMISH CHAPERONE

Colorado Amish Courtships • by Leigh Bale

After an accident leaves her injured, Amish schoolteacher Caroline Schwartz needs assistance…but Ben Yoder is the last person she expects the bishop to ask. With Ben's dark past, many avoid him, but as he helps Caroline care for her orphaned little cousins, she might just realize he's her perfect match.

CHILD ON HIS DOORSTEP

Rescue Haven • by Lee Tobin McClain

Suddenly a father after a toddler's abandoned on his doorstep, Corbin Beck has no idea how to care for a little boy. But town troublemaker Samantha Alcorn is looking to turn over a new leaf…and hiring her as his live-in nanny could solve both their problems.

RAISING HONOR

Colorado Grooms • by Jill Lynn

When Ryker Hayes learns his niece has been put into foster care, he's determined to become her guardian…even if it means moving to Colorado. But as he begins supervised visits with little Honor, might her foster mother, Charlie Brightwood, become another reason to stick around for good?

READY TO TRUST

Hearts of Oklahoma • by Tina Radcliffe

Splitting her inheritance with Reece Rainbolt complicates things for Claire Ballard —especially since he's the father of her secret daughter. He'll buy her half of the family ranch only on one condition: she must stay in town to help with the harvest…and let him get to know his little girl.

THE ORPHANS' BLESSING

by Lorraine Beatty

Finally tracking down her long-lost sister only to find she's passed away, Sophie Armstrong wants to connect with the only family she has left—her orphaned nieces and nephew. As she bonds with the children, can she win over their uncle Zach Conrad's trust…and possibly his heart?

FALLING FOR THE INNKEEPER

by Meghann Whistler

Single mom Laura Lessoway won't give in to her mother's plan of selling her late grandmother's inn without a fight. But when attorney Jonathan Masters arrives to arrange an offer from his client, she's drawn to him. With his career and her home on the line, can they ever find common ground?
